HARD TIMES ON A
SOUTHERN CHAIN GANG

SOUTHERN CLASSICS SERIES

Mark M. Smith and Peggy G. Hargis, Series Editors

HARD TIMES ON A
SOUTHERN CHAIN GANG

Originally Published as the Novel
Georgia Nigger (1932)

JOHN L. SPIVAK
New Introduction by David A. Davis

The University of South Carolina Press

*Published in Cooperation with the Institute for
Southern Studies of the University of South Carolina*

New introductory material
© 2012 University of South Carolina

Cloth edition published by
Brewer, Warren and Putnam, 1932
Paperback edition published by
the University of South Carolina Press,
Columbia, South Carolina 29208

www.sc.edu/uscpress

Manufactured in the United States of America

21 20 19 18 17 16 15 14 13 12
10 9 8 7 6 5 4 3 2 1

Library of Congress Cataloging-in-Publication Data
Spivak, John L. (John Louis), 1897–1981.
[Georgia Nigger]
Hard times on a Southern chain gang / John L. Spivak ;
new introduction by David A. Davis.
p. cm. — (Southern classics series)
"Originally published as the novel Georgia Nigger (1932)."
". . .On the Chain Gang (reproduced in an
appendix in this volume) . . ."—Preface.
"Published in cooperation with the Institute for
Southern Studies of the University of South Carolina."
ISBN 978-1-61117-044-3 (pbk : alk. paper)
1. African Americans—Fiction. 2. Chain gangs—Fiction.
3. Georgia—Fiction. I. Davis, David A. (David
Alexander), 1975– II. Title.
PS3537.P7446G46 2012
813'.52—dc22
2011031535

This book was printed on recycled paper with 30 percent
postconsumer waste content.

Publication of the Southern Classics series is
made possible in part by the generous support
of the Watson-Brown Foundation.

CONTENTS

SERIES EDITORS' PREFACE

In 1930 and early 1931 a left-leaning journalist by the name of John L. Spivak investigated Georgia's prisons, work camps, and chain gangs. He interviewed officials, photographed conditions, spoke with inmates, and examined documents produced by the Georgia Prison Commission. His investigation exposed a simple but brutal truth: debt peonage, convict leasing, and chain gangs constituted a constellation of involuntary servitude. Georgia's penal system, replete with racism, corruption, and greed, was supplying the state and wealthy planters with a steady stream of cheap labor. Spivak, who had a reputation for experimenting with new forms of reporting, opted to forgo more traditional routes of publication for his report. He chose instead to expose the cruel reality of an unjust and inhumane penal system by cloaking facts in fiction. Perhaps he thought a novel about a black sharecropper would make a bitter pill easier to swallow, especially if he suspected that white or privileged audiences would prefer to remain ignorant and unseeing.

Originally published in 1932 (with the provocative and unflattering title *Georgia Nigger*) Spivak's novel will resonate with today's students and scholars of the American South. Not only do we see the caustic reality of a southern penal system during the early decades of the twentieth century through the eyes of our protagonist, David Jackson, but we are presented with an insightful new introduction by David A. Davis and a reprint of a pamphlet written by Spivak that describes his research—additions that will help make this classic a valued resource for decades to come.

Southern Classics returns to general circulation books of importance dealing with the history and culture of the American South. Sponsored by the Institute for Southern Studies, the series is advised by a board of distinguished scholars who suggest titles and editors of individual volumes to the series editors and help establish priorities in publication.

Chronological age alone does not determine a title's designation as a Southern Classic. The criteria also include significance in contributing to a broad understanding of the region, timeliness in relation to events and moments of peculiar interest to the American South, usefulness in the classroom, and suitability for inclusion in personal and institutional collections on the region.

MARK M. SMITH
PEGGY G. HARGIS
Series Editors

INTRODUCTION

THE CIRCUMSTANCES OF DAVID JACKSON'S LIFE are beyond his control. Born into a black sharecropping family in Georgia in the early twentieth century, his only viable occupation is to provide manual labor, deferentially cultivating cotton for white landowners. In the Jim Crow South, an elaborate system of social, legal, and economic forces limit his freedom and exploit his labor. His story illustrates that living conditions for black laborers had not improved substantially in the seventy years since the abolition of slavery. John L. Spivak first published this novel in 1932 to draw attention to the thousands of black men who suffered or died as a result of the outrageously inhumane conditions of the southern chain gangs, and it exposes a broader network of racist power structures involving sharecropping, paternalism, debt peonage, and corrupt politicians that trapped men in hopeless menial labor. David Jackson, the book's main character, is a metaphor for race and labor in the South, and Spivak used him to portray the South as the site of a complex set of social problems. The novel has a social message; indeed it was intended to be a vehicle for social change in the 1930s, but its message is still relevant.

Spivak sought to focus public attention on chain gangs to create an outcry to abolish them. As he explained in the book itself, he did not intend to limit his indictment to Georgia, which did "not stand alone as a state lost to fundamental justice and humanity."[1] Georgia was meant to represent all the southern states that used chain gangs as a form of incarceration. For several months during 1930 and 1931, Spivak investigated the Georgia Prison Commission and the chain gang system. He interviewed officials, purloined documents, visited camps, spoke with guards and inmates, and took photographs. As a journalist he would ordinarily have used this material to write either a nonfiction book or a series of newspaper articles, but he chose to write this book as a novel. That choice makes this book interesting both as a documentary record of sharecropping, chain gangs, and debt peonage and as an imaginative projection of black life in the South.

The book's original title, *Georgia Nigger*, is provocative and problematic, especially for contemporary readers. In the context of 1930s America, the word "nigger" was used frequently in mainstream discourse, often as a hateful or demeaning racial epithet. Randall Kennedy explains that the word is America's "paradigmatic slur" and that it has a complicated legacy, especially in literature and popular culture, as the recent debate over an expurgated version of Mark Twain's *Adventures of Huckleberry Finn* demonstrates.[2] Joseph Conrad's novel *The Nigger of the Narcissus* has from time to time been removed from library shelves, and Carl Van Vechten's novel *Nigger Heaven,* published six years before Spivak's novel, was highly controversial. Spivak understood the term's significance, and he chose it deliberately, perhaps to highlight the plight that David Jackson endures as a result of his abject position. The title was shocking when the book was published, and the *Daily Worker,* the Communist newspaper that serialized the book, published the following disclaimer with each installment of the book: "*Georgia Nigger* is the name of a book. The white ruling class term 'nigger' is not used by *The Daily Worker.* We are unfortunately compelled to use the term because of copyright requirements. The author himself is not sympathetic to the term, but used it in order to bring forth the degrading system which operates against Negroes."[3] The title serves a purpose, not to demean the black person, but to implicate the system that dehumanizes him. Readers should find the term unsettling, as it is supposed to be, but they should also recognize that Spivak used it intentionally, not casually. This edition uses a more descriptive and less controversial title to appeal to contemporary readers, but it does not change his text, and it recognizes that Spivak used the term deliberately.

Spivak became interested in chain gangs through the course of his career as a muckraking journalist. He was born into a working-class Jewish family in New Haven, Connecticut, in 1897, and he began writing for newspapers while still in high school. He worked a series of factory jobs, where he developed sympathy for exploited workers, before taking a full-time job as a reporter. In the 1920s he wrote for papers in New York and for several leftist papers, including the *Call,* the *Daily Worker,* and *New Masses.* His first major story covered the battle of Matewan in May 1920, a skirmish that erupted in West Virginia when hired detectives from the Baldwin-Felts Agency attempted to evict coal miners who were organizing for the United Mine Workers of America. Several people were killed in the incident, which marked a pivotal moment in American labor history. Spivak also covered the controversial trial of Nicola Sacco and Bartolomeo Vanzetti, Italian anarchists accused of murder and robbery in Massachusetts. Later in the 1920s he reported on the rise of fascism in Europe, and his work on socialist and antifascist causes earned him the title "America's Greatest Reporter" from *Time* magazine, while muck-raking reporter Lincoln Steffens called him "the best of us."[4]

In 1930 he turned his attention to the living conditions of African Americans in the South. He had come across an article about a chain gang in North Carolina that inspired him to learn more about the southern penal system. Before encountering the article on chain gangs, he had thought of himself as reasonably well informed about conditions in the South, and he took for granted that black people were exploited as part of the normal social order. As he began studying race, labor, and southern history, he realized that historians brought their own racial biases to their explanations of racial conditions in the South. "Slowly," he wrote, "I formed a picture of the conditions millions of Negroes lived under in the Deep South. Three quarters of a century after they had been technically set free, some of them were still being confined in cages like animals. I was discovering an America about which I knew nothing."[5]

He went to the office of the Georgia Prison Commission at the state capitol in Atlanta, where he developed a cordial yet uneasy relationship with Vivian Stanley, the prison commissioner. He persuaded Stanley to allow him to read the commission's annual reports, and he gained access to punishment reports and death certificates. At tremendous risk he stole some examples of these reports by slipping them into a newspaper and sneaking them out of the building and had copies made of them. The reports, called Official Whipping Reports, document the names of convicts, their punishment, and the reason for the punishment—disobeying camp rules, impudence, loafing, or attempting escape.[6] In 1931 the Georgia prison camps stopped the practice of whipping as a punishment, so restricted movement for a period of time, usually no more than one hour, became the primary means of punishment. To add credibility to the events of the novel, Spivak included images of these reports in the appendix to the book. After much cajoling, he persuaded Commissioner Stanley to sign a general letter of introduction granting him permission to visit prison camps in the state and allowing him to speak to wardens, guards, and inmates.

His first visit was to the Dougherty County prison camp near Albany, Georgia. When he arrived, he witnessed the restricted movement punishment that prisoners endured. An inmate's legs were tied to a post, his hands were cuffed, and a rope was run through the cuffs. The rope was wrapped around a bar attached to a building several feet away, and the rope was pulled tight until the inmate was bent over at the waist and his arms were pulled as far forward as possible. He was supposed to be held in this posture for an hour, but most men passed out before the hour was up. Using Commissioner Stanley's letter to gain access, Spivak was able to photograph this punishment and to tour the grounds with the warden, a political appointee, who explained the inmates' living conditions, made casually racist comments, and spat tobacco juice on the ground. He repeated this process for weeks, visiting camps throughout the state and developing an exhaustive record of gross inhumanity under the guise of justice.

In Americus, Georgia, he interviewed Sumter County warden C. H. Wheatley, who gave him a practical explanation of the chain gang system. Sheriffs and their deputies, he explained, work on a fee schedule that gave them a monetary incentive to make arrests. The local courts and prosecuting attorneys, who received no salary, were paid from court costs and fees levied against defendants. The apparatus of justice, thus, had an overt financial incentive in arresting and convicting people. The positions of sheriff, judge, and prosecutor were elected positions, so the officeholders also had an incentive to ingratiate themselves with voters. As blacks could not vote in the South, they were completely helpless before the justice system. Black men who could not pay fines levied against them could be sentenced to the chain gang for exorbitant periods of time to work off their sentence.

Men who were either convicted of a crime or unable to pay a fine would be sent to a chain gang to work under the supervision of a warden, Wheatley explained. The warden supervised walking bosses who ran work gangs, guards who carried shotguns at all times, and cooks who fed the prisoners. The prisoners worked from before dawn until dusk every weekday and half a day on Saturdays. They had the opportunity to take a bath on Saturday and to see visitors on Sunday. The inmates received no pay for their work, but the county collected taxes for public works projects and charged fees for private projects. The system was generally profitable for the state, and there was a strong impetus to incarcerate able-bodied men.

The appearance of Spivak's book coincided with another incident that focused national attention on Georgia chain gangs. In 1932, just before the publication of *Georgia Nigger*, Robert E. Burns published his sensational autobiography, *I Am a Fugitive from a Georgia Chain Gang!*[7] In 1922 Burns, a white World War I veteran from New York, was arrested in Atlanta for petty robbery and sentenced to ten years on the chain gang. He escaped and had a successful career in publishing in Chicago until his estranged wife turned him in. He was returned to the chain gang in 1929 and escaped again the following year. He then made his way to New Jersey and published his story. Warner Brothers adapted the book into a blockbuster film starring Paul Muni. When Georgia officials arrested Burns again at a film screening in New Jersey, the governor of New Jersey took the unusual step of holding an extradition hearing in Burns's case. Spivak testified at the hearing, recounting the treatment of inmates he had witnessed in Georgia and sharing the prison documents and photographs from his own research. The governor denied the request for extradition, allowing Burns to remain in New Jersey.

Spivak's novel was published amid the furor surrounding the Burns case. Initially the book was serialized in the *Daily Worker,* the newspaper of the American Communist Party. Spivak had offered the novel to *American Mercury, Survey Graphic,* and the *Chicago Defender,* a leading African American newspaper, all of whom passed on it. The *Daily Worker* published it because it fit with their agenda to inspire revolution among the oppressed African Americans and poor whites in the South, but as Alex Lichtenstein observed, there was a "considerable gap between Spivak's political analysis of the chain gang and the Communist Party's preferred interpretation."[8] The party's viewpoint differed from Spivak's presentation of African American religion, paternalistic class relations, and with the sense of individualism displayed by David Jackson. Truthfully, other than the fact that the novel was serialized in the *Daily Worker* in thirty-six installments during November and December of 1932, it was no more socialist than many other examples of Depression-era documentary writing. It was also published in abbreviated format in the *Des Moines Tribune,* and an excerpt was published in *Crisis.* The Labor Research Association, a pro-union group, published a pamphlet, *On the Chain Gang* (reproduced in an appendix in this volume), in which Spivak describes his research for the novel.[9] Brewer, Warren and Putnam published the book in 1932, and it was also published in England in 1933.[10] It received mostly positive reviews in northern and midwestern newspapers, including the *New York Times,* which noted that it had "the weight and authority of a sociological investigation."[11] Arthur Raper, a sociologist who studied the conditions of rural southern poverty, described the book in his *New Republic* review as "documented melodrama" and asserted that "the conditions depicted reflect great discredit on our whole civilization."[12] African American poet and scholar Sterling Brown described it as "a second *Uncle Tom's Cabin,* an indictment of peonage and convict-labor in Georgia, powerful enough to put to shame all the rhapsodists of the folk Negro's happy state."[13]

xiv INTRODUCTION

Southern newspapers gave the book a less positive reception, and it created considerable controversy in Georgia. Spivak's book garnered significantly less attention than Burns's case, but the American Civil Liberties Union used it to level accusations of "cruel and inhuman punishments" against the Georgia Prison Commission. An open letter published in several newspapers and signed by twelve prominent persons, including Broadus Mitchell, Ellen Glasgow, and James Weldon Johnson, threatened legal action in federal courts.[14] The *Atlanta Constitution* ran an article in response, quoting Vivian Stanley, who alleged that Spivak had posed as a federal agent to gain access to the chain gangs and that he had paid inmates to pose for staged photographs.[15] Spivak denied the allegations and pointed out that a warden appears in one of the photographs showing an inmate being punished.[16]

The controversy dissipated quickly. The ACLU never brought a suit to court, and even in the wake of the negative attention brought by the Burns case, the Georgia Prison Commission did not reform the chain gang system. Spivak gave talks about his book and the system in several cities, but even he lost hope that the system would be changed. He became sanguine, remarking that "the country as a whole was indifferent" to the condition of southern blacks on the chain gang.[17] The following year Spivak covered the International Labor Defense's appeal of the Scottsboro boys' conviction on rape charges in Alabama, and he was unsurprised when the nine black men were ultimately convicted in spite of a flimsy case.

After 1933 Spivak left the South and shifted his focus to anti-Semitism, Nazism, government corruption, and international politics. His book *The Shrine of the Silver Dollar* (1940) contributed to the downfall of Father Charles Coughlin, the anti-Semitic priest with a popular radio broadcast. As a result of the Red Scare of the 1950s, however, Spivak was forced to write under a series of pen names, including Howard Booth, Paul Dinsmore, and Monroe Fry, publishing salacious articles in men's magazine such as *Esquire, Cavalier,* and *Male to Male.* Over the course of his career, he published twelve books, including his autobiography, *A Man in His Time* (1967). He died in 1981 at the age of eighty-four. He had been married to his wife, Mabel, for sixty-four years, and they had a daughter and a grandson.

SPIVAK'S BOOK HAD A NEGLIGIBLE EFFECT on the chain gang system, except for bringing some attention to the plight of black southerners in the South. Spivak, however, was not the first person to criticize the southern system of justice publicly. In 1885 George Washington Cable described the convict lease program that preceded the chain gang as "evil" because it exploited convicts for profit.[18] These comments and other racially progressive writings made Cable unwelcome in the South, but the notion of the South as stubbornly racist and in opposition to the mainstream of American liberal democracy became a recurring theme in American writing. In *Darker Phases of the South,* for example, Frank Tannenbaum listed southern prisons, alongside the Ku Klux Klan and economic dependence on cotton, as a major social problem in the South.[19] By the time Spivak wrote his novel about chain gangs, the exploitation of inmates for labor had become an entrenched component of the racist southern social structure.

The state-sponsored use of inmates for labor developed during Reconstruction as southerners reconfigured the region's economic and social structures in the wake of emancipation.[20] The Thirteenth Amendment to the U.S. Constitution abolished slavery "except as a punishment for crime whereof the party shall have been duly convicted." The "punishment for crime" clause allowed for the possibility of involuntary servitude for certain individuals deemed to be criminals. From 1865 to 1877, when the U.S. government occupied the southern states, former slaves were allowed to vote and hold political office, and the Freedmen's Bureau represented the economic and political interests of African Americans. After the Compromise of 1877, however, federal troops withdrew from the South, and white southerners returned to political control. This was a politically unstable period for African Americans throughout the South. After the war most southern states passed a series of laws, known as Black Codes, that restricted the social mobility and economic agency of African Americans.[21] Vagrancy laws, for example, allowed local police to jail anyone who could not prove employment, and false pretense laws prevented anyone in one person's employ from negotiating employment with another person. Laws were written that created crimes for which poor blacks could be arrested and held in involuntary servitude.

During the Reconstruction era the southern economy revived, but it still depended on the manual cultivation of cotton, tobacco, and other staple crops. Property was not redistributed after the Civil War; the federal government returned confiscated lands to the previous owners. Antebellum plantation owners, therefore, still owned the bulk of productive lands, and they attempted several labor arrangements to cultivate their crops. One of the initial attempts replicated the gang-labor methods of the antebellum plantation with laborers working on wage pay contracts, often brokered by the Freedmen's Bureau. Lack of currency and fears that laborers would break contracts led many plantation owners to pay laborers a portion of the crop produced. However, as Roger Ransom and Richard Sutch noted, the wage system "bore an uneasy resemblance to slavery."[22] In time the share tenancy arrangement emerged as the dominant system of labor in the South.[23] A landowner entered into a contract with a laborer to farm a plot of land and to divide the crop at harvest. The laborer's rent would be paid in the form of a lien against the expected crop, and the laborer would receive any proceeds remaining after the rent and any other charges were deducted. The system allowed for egregious abuses, and laborers often found their families in debt after the crop had been divided and sold.

In Spivak's novel David Jackson is the son of a sharecropper. His father, the son of slaves, annually signs a contract that he cannot read with Shay Pearson, a white landowner. The contract stipulates that Pearson will provide "a mule, seed, and a monthly advance of twelve dollars between February and August inclusive, in return for half his crop after all advances and interest thereon were deducted" (33). Pearson charges 18 percent interest on advances, and his sharecroppers never pay their debt according to his accounting. As a result of this contract, Pearson essentially owns the Jackson family's labor because "Georgia law provided that as long as [Jackson] owed the planter one dollar he could not leave the Pearson farm without facing arrest and the chain gang for swindling" (34).

At the same time the sharecropping system evolved in the wake of emancipation, the southern penal system redeveloped after the war.[24] Before the war all southern states had penitentiaries that incarcerated inmates in seclusion. Many of these penitentiaries operated prison industries, but few of the industries were profitable and most inmates were white men. In the antebellum South, masters had authority to punish their slaves, who were rarely punished by the state. By the end of the Civil War, most southern penitentiaries were empty—their inmates released to fight in last ditch defenses of the Confederacy—and the states had few resources available to rebuild prisons. But states had an urgent mandate to enforce the Black Codes and to regulate freedmen. States began leasing convicts to private companies to work on railroads, in mines and factories, and on plantations to generate revenue. Under the arrangement the company was supposed to provide the inmates' food, shelter, and medical care in exchange for their labor.[25] The system gave states a financial incentive to incarcerate men; it gave companies a legal means to employ men in involuntary servitude; and it provided no oversight to safeguard the inmate's welfare, which allowed men to be overworked, starved, and beaten. In *Slavery by Another Name,* Douglas Blackmon documents that thousands of men died working in horrendous conditions.

Progressive-era reforms led to the end of convict leasing, but not to the end of the exploitation of convicts. In 1908 Georgia governor Hoke Smith, who had investigated cases of inmate brutality two decades earlier, ended the leasing of inmates in part because industries that leased convicts were financially destabilized in the Panic of 1907 and in part because human rights abuses had become public. Over the next twenty years other southern states followed suit, and they instead employed convicts in public works. Southern politicians campaigned on platforms of improving roads, which was to speed the movement of agricultural goods to market and to increase business. They proposed to minimize the fiscal impact of the projects by using convict labor. Alex Lichtenstein claimed that "progressive reformers relied on the chain gang to reclaim what they saw as the state's 'government duty' simultaneously to constrain and uplift the black race; unfortunately, in the process the 'sufferings of the convict' were ignored."[26] Chain gangs transferred the systematic exploitation of inmates from private companies to state and local governments.

Spivak's book depicts conditions in county work camps. Buzzard's Roost, the camp in fictional Chickasaw County, is based on a typical camp where misdemeanor offenders work on highway projects. Spivak noted that counties often deliberately convicted alleged criminals of minor offenses so that they would remain within the county of sentence because felony offenders were processed through the state prison commission and redistributed to the counties in proportion to their population. Keeping inmates within the county increased the number of available laborers. A key difference between convict leasing and chain gangs, as Spivak made clear, was that, whereas convict leasing was a means of generating revenue, chain gangs were a system of political patronage. Commissioners, wardens, and doctors were all political appointees, usually with no penological experience and no one overseeing their work. Inmates on chain gangs were at the mercy of the wardens, who had extensive authority to withhold food or medical care and to mete out corporal punishment, and they had little recourse to appeal their sentences or their living conditions.

In addition to chain gangs, Spivak's book depicts another form of involuntary servitude, debt peonage. In one scene a landowner, Jim Deering, conspires with the county sheriff to arrest David and several other young men on dubious charges. Deering arranges to pay the men's fines and then forces them to work off their debt on his plantation. In *The Shadow of Slavery: Peonage in the South, 1901–1969,* Pete Daniel asserted that "peonage infected the South like a cancer, eating away at the economic freedom of blacks, driving the poor whites to work harder in order to compete with virtual slave labor, and preserving the class structure inherited from slavery days."[27] Peons were bound into debt either through the means Deering uses or, more commonly, through exorbitant interest charged on goods purchased through furnish merchants—often the landowners' commissaries—from whom laborers were forced to purchase food, fertilizer, and supplies. Peonage technically violated the Thirteenth Amendment, but even when federal courts ruled against the practice, it persisted as part of the region's complex set of labor relations after slavery.

Spivak's book exposed a broad set of human rights abuses in the South. At various points the region's progressive politicians and civil rights leaders made attempts to reform elements of the system. One of the most significant was Georgia governor Ellis Arnall's attempt to reform the penal system in 1943. He convened a special session of legislature, advocated rehabilitation over punishment, and created a Department of Corrections to replace the State Prison Commission.[28] He requested that the Board of Parole and Pardons grant a parole to Robert Burns, and he personally represented Burns at his final hearing in 1945. His gestures, however, did not end the chain gang system.

Southern states continued to use chain gangs until the 1960s. They became less common after World War II, but not necessarily because southerners became more enlightened about human rights abuses. Rather the prevalence of heavy machinery made manual labor for highway construction and maintenance impractical, and federal highway grants explicitly stipulated that convict labor could not be used on public works projects. States constructed more penitentiaries for long-term incarceration, county work camps became less cost effective, and by 1970 many of the Black Code laws either had been repealed or were superseded by civil rights legislation. Occasionally politicians have proposed or implemented convict labor programs in the recent past, but chain gangs such as the one David Jackson served on remain an ignominious part of the South's racist history.[29]

The practice of sharecropping yielded to similar economic forces.[30] One farmer with a tractor could work more land than several families without one, so maintaining a large labor force became unnecessary. The mechanization of cotton production lagged behind other forms of agricultural production because it took a relatively long time to develop a reliable mechanical cotton picker, but between the 1940s and 1960s most sharecropping families either left or were removed from the farms where they worked. Many migrated to southern cities or to cities outside the South.[31] However, even by the time of the civil rights movement, thousands of rural African Americans continued to work on shares, deferentially cultivating cotton and other staple crops as generations of their ancestors had.

IN ADDITION TO THE FICTIONAL STORY of David Jackson, Spivak's book includes a number of photographs of chain gang inmates in desperate conditions. During the Great Depression several other books were published that combined text and images to document the suffering of poor or powerless people. In such books as James Agee and Walker Evans's *Let Us Now Praise Famous Men,* Erskine Caldwell and Margaret Bourke-White's *You Have Seen Their Faces,* Dorothea Lange and Paul S. Taylor's *An American Exodus,* Archibald MacLeish's *Land of the Free,* and Richard Wright and Edwin Rosskam's *Twelve Million Black Voices,* photographs and nonfiction prose combine to focus public attention on social ills. Many of the photographers who collaborated on these texts were also part of the Farm Security Administration, a federal agency that employed photographers to document poverty in America's rural areas to generate political support for New Deal legislation.[32] These texts pressed both a social and an aesthetic agenda, simultaneously recording and making art out of American poverty.[33]

Spivak stipulated that the characters in the book were fictitious, but he felt "an appendix of pictures and documents . . . necessary" (xxvii) to establish the work's credibility. He explained that he took the photographs himself and that the documents "are but a few of the many gathering dust in the State Capitol in Atlanta" (xxvii). The photographs and documents in the appendix mirror and amplify the novel's plot. Beyond authenticating Spivak's representation of the chain gang, the photographs indict the chain gang as a depraved, inhumane form of punishment. In some cases the photographs overshadow the fiction. The photograph captioned "A Halter for the Neck," for example, shows an inmate from Muscogee County sitting on the front steps of a bunkhouse. Behind him the crosshatch pattern of bars forms a background that blends with the horizontal pattern of stripes on his uniform. The linear patterns contrast with the sinuous chains connecting his ankles to a metal collar around his neck, which "suggests a noose."[34] The bars, stripes, and chains dehumanize the convict, forcing the viewer to reconcile his expressive hands and face with the symbols of incarceration.

In *Documentary Expression and Thirties America,* William Stott argued that Spivak's book allowed the reader to have a vicarious experience of the chain gang. He contended that Spivak "used photographs to ·persuade his audience directly that convicts were kept in shackles and forced to suffer cruel and unusual punishment. But the photos, though they made the exposé credible, did not give it its passion; they documented facts rather than feelings."[35] As documents of torture, the photographs allow the reader to visualize atrocity, which, Barbie Zelizer warned, could have the effect of normalizing it.[36] In this case, however, "the gaze of Spivak's camera reflects that of a Foucauldian panopticon. In Spivak's case, the eye abhorred what it saw and sought change."[37] The interplay of the photographs and the documents with the novel's plot has a powerful, highly unsettling effect on the reader. Even if the reader can rationalize the novel as a work of fiction, the photographs bring the uncomfortable reality of the chain gang into sharp focus.

This leads to a difficult question about Spivak's book. Why did he write it as a novel? Spivak was a journalist, and he wrote several books of reportage over the course of his career, but this is his only novel. Considering the amount of research he did for the book, he had enough material to write a powerful nonfiction exposé, but he felt that a work of fiction would have a broader impact. He decided to write it as a novel, he explained, "because to indict state after state, chain gang camp after camp in so many southern states would have necessitated even greater research than I had given it (two years). It would also have been repetitious to detail conditions which existed in Georgia, Florida, the Carolinas, etc. with overwhelming evidence. In novel form I could say, as I did in a brief introduction, that the conditions described exist in many southern states; Georgia was simply an example. I used the photographs I had personally taken because that was visual evidence of what otherwise might not be believed by well meaning southerners, many of whom were shocked when they did see them."[38]

The tension between the book's fictional plot and its journalistic technique complicated it for many readers. Alex Lichtenstein noted that some readers took it "as a thinly varnished piece of reportage, and regarded its aesthetic pretensions as so much window dressing. In the cultural climate of 1932, however, this was grounds for praise rather than indictment."[39] According to Walter Rideout, books that portrayed "the human suffering imposed by some socioeconomic system and advocated that the system be fundamentally changed" were common between 1900 and 1950.[40] Spivak's novel juggles its social and its aesthetic agendas, and it is difficult to assess if either was entirely successful. It received generally high critical praise, and it generated some controversy, although Burn's sensational story overshadowed it. But it evidently did not sell well: it had fallen out of print, and it has received scant scholarly attention, at least so far. In spite of these facts, however, Spivak's novel deserves reappraisal.

Although not a great novel, the book has some compelling literary merit. Its technique demonstrates many elements of literary naturalism, particularly in the sense that environmental factors determine the characters' fate and in the sympathetic presentation of the characters. Spivak portrays David Jackson as a victim, not a criminal. Although he is arrested three times, he never commits an actual crime. Spivak further balances his victimization with acts of resistance, specifically his escape from Deering's plantation and his futile attempt to escape from Buzzard's Roost. The antagonist in the book is the broad set of social forces that virtually enslave David Jackson. White characters, such as the landowners, the sheriff, and the wardens, represent these forces, but they too are controlled by the forces, not in control of them. Spivak incorporates some recurring symbols into the story that enhance the characterization. The most prominent symbol is a cross that appears on both the first page of the novel—"two lanterns hung from the wooden cross driven deep in the red soil of the convict camp stockade" (1)—and on the last page of the novel—"from his bunk he could see the tiny red ants scurrying in all directions and the shadow of the cross dark on the red soil" (241). The cross has obvious Christian overtones; it suggests that David Jackson represents a sacrifice, and it allows for the possibility of redemption.

The book's aesthetic characteristics are important, but the book is most significant for its historical veracity. Although chain gangs have disappeared, Spivak's book details how the prison industrial complex developed in the early-twentieth-century South. And the dynamics of incarceration that Spivak described continue to resonate in contemporary prison culture. The United States incarcerates a higher percentage of its population than any other country, and poor black men are disproportionately represented in the prison population.[41] In contemporary Georgia almost one-third of all adult black men have been incarcerated, paroled, or placed on probation. In 2010 the inmates at several prisons in Georgia coordinated a strike to protest inhumane conditions. They requested wages for the work they performed in prison industries, an end to cruel and unusual punishments, and decent living conditions.[42] The strike was brief, but it highlighted that, even though the outrageous conditions of the chain gang have been replaced with modern penitentiaries,

America's prison system could be much more equitable and humane.[43]

Michel Foucault described the evolution of the modern prison in *Discipline and Punish: The Birth of the Prison,* focusing on the incarceration of the body as a site of power relations.[44] As a carceral system the chain gang mediates between systems that made spectacles of public torture and the modern carceral system that obscures convicts from the public. Chain gangs in the South combined methods of corporal punishment that had been common in the early-nineteenth-century system of justice with the labor conditions of slavery to create a system that utterly degraded inmates. Spivak's book invites us to reconsider the system's relationship to labor and poverty in southern history and how the intertwining of race, labor, and incarceration in the United States continues to present a complex set of social problems.

I am grateful to Mark Smith, Douglas Blackmon, Matthew Mancini, William Stott, Alex Lichtenstein, Peter Caster, and especially Gene Gorman for their support and advice on this project. I am also deeply grateful to the students in my southern justice class at Mercer University for discussing the complex problems of race and incarceration with me.

The Special Collections Research Center at Syracuse University Library and the Harry Ransom Center at the University of Texas provided access to Spivak's papers. A Griffith Grant and funding from the Mercer University College of Liberal Arts supported research on this project.

NOTES

1. John L. Spivak, *Hard Times on a Southern Chain Gang* (Columbia: University of South Carolina Press, 2012), xxvii. Citations are hereafter given parenthetically in text. Originally published as *Georgia Nigger* (New York: Brewer, Warren and Putnam, 1932).

2. Randall Kennedy, *Nigger: The Strange Career of a Troublesome Word* (New York: Pantheon, 2002), 27.

3. This disclaimer comes from the *Daily Worker,* October 27, 1932, but it was used with virtually all references to the book published in the newspaper.

4. William Stott discusses Spivak's reputation in *Documentary Expression in Thirties America* (New York: Oxford University Press, 1973), 34.

5. John L. Spivak, *A Man in His Time* (New York: Horizon Press, 1967), 167.

6. The actual documents that he took can be found among his papers at the Harry Ransom Center at the University of Texas at Austin.

7. Robert Burns's case captivated America, and one could easily conclude that his case was remarkable not because he experienced human rights abuses, but

because he was a white northerner trapped in system designed primarily for black southerners. For more information, see his autobiography, *I Am a Fugitive from a Georgia Chain Gang!* (1932; repr., Athens: University of Georgia Press, 1997), and his brother's self-righteous account of the case, Vincent Godfrey Burns, *The Man Who Broke a Thousand Chains; The Story of Social Reformation of the Prisons of the South* (Washington, D.C.: Acropolis Books, 1968).

8. Alex Lichtenstein, "Chain Gangs, Communism, and the 'Negro Question': John L. Spivak's *Georgia Nigger*," *Georgia Historical Quarterly* 79 (Fall 1995): 642.

9. *Des Moines Tribune,* November 23, 1932; "The Convict Camp at Buzzard's Roost," *Crisis* 39 (October 1932): 318 and 332; and *On the Chain Gang* (New York: International Publishers, 1932).

10. The British edition was published by Wishart and Company in 1933. Paterson Smith of Montclair, New Jersey, published a reprint edition in 1969.

11. Unsigned review of *Georgia Nigger,* by John L. Spivak. *New York Times Book Review,* October 16, 1932.

12. Arthur Raper, "After Slavery," *New Republic* 37, no. 22 (1932): 77.

13. Sterling A. Brown, "Negro Character as Seen by White Authors," *Journal of Negro Education* 2 (April 1933): 202–3.

14. "The Civil Liberties Union Files Charges of Cruelty," *New York Times,* November 20, 1932.

15. "Life-Termer Bribed to Pose for Spivak Book, Says Stanley," *Atlanta Constitution,* November 22, 1932.

16. "John L. Spivak Responds to Commissioner Stanley," *Savannah News,* November 23, 1932.

17. Spivak, *A Man in His Time,* 191.

18. George Washington Cable, *"The Silent South," Together with "The Freedman's Case in Equity" and "The Convict Lease System"* (New York: C. Scribner's Sons, 1885), 122.

19. Frank Tannenbaum, *Darker Phases of the South* (New York: G. P. Putnam's Sons, 1924).

20. For explanations of Reconstruction, especially as it affected black life in the South, see Eric Foner, *Reconstruction: America's Unfinished Revolution, 1863–1877* (New York: Harper & Row, 1988); Leon F. Litwack, *Been in the Storm So Long: The Aftermath of Slavery* (New York: Vintage, 1979); and Susan Eva O'Donovan, *Becoming Free in the Cotton South* (Cambridge, Mass.: Harvard University Press, 2007).

21. For a history of the Black Codes, see Theodore Wilson, *The Black Codes of the South* (University: University of Alabama Press, 1965).

22. Roger L. Ransom and Richard Sutch, *One Kind of Freedom: The Economic Consequences of Emancipation* (New York: Cambridge University Press, 1977), 65.

23. For additional studies on the origins of southern sharecropping, see Jay R. Mandle, *The Roots of Black Poverty: The Southern Plantation Economy after*

the Civil War (Durham, N.C.: Duke University Press, 1978), and Edward Royce, *The Origins of Southern Sharecropping* (Philadelphia: Temple University Press, 1993).

24. Edward L. Ayers documents the early history of the southern justice system in *Vengeance and Justice: Crime and Punishment in the 19th Century American South* (New York: Oxford University Press, 1984).

25. Key studies of convict leasing and labor include Douglas Blackmon, *Slavery by Another Name: The Re-enslavement of Black Americans from the Civil War to World War II* (New York: Anchor Books, 2009); Alex Lichtenstein, *Twice the Work of Free Labor: The Political Economy of Convict Labor in the New South* (New York: Verso, 1996); David M. Oshinsky, *Worse Than Slavery: Parchman Farm and the Ordeal of Jim Crow Justice* (New York: Free Press, 1996); and Matthew J. Mancini, *One Dies, Get Another: Convict Leasing in the American South, 1866–1928* (Columbia: University of South Carolina Press, 1996).

26. Lichtenstein, *Twice the Work of Free Labor,* 168.

27. Pete Daniel, *The Shadow of Slavery: Peonage in the South, 1901–1969* (Urbana: University of Illinois Press, 1972), 11.

28. Harold Paulk Henderson, *The Politics of Change in Georgia: A Political Biography of Ellis Arnall* (Athens: University of Georgia Press, 1991), 63–76.

29. The term "chain gangs" has been used in a few recent contexts to describe prison work details, notably in Alabama in 1995 and in Maricopa County, Arizona. In American prisons inmates routinely work either in industries located within the penitentiary or on community work programs. Some prison activists continue to call for the abolition of the modern prison system; see, for example, Angela Y. Davis, *Are Prisons Obsolete?* (New York: Seven Stories Press, 2003).

30. For histories of agricultural change during the twentieth century, see Gilbert C. Fite, *Cotton Fields No More: Southern Agriculture, 1865–1980* (Lexington: University Press of Kentucky, 1984); Jack Temple Kirby, *Rural Worlds Lost: The American South, 1920–1960* (Baton Rouge: Louisiana State University Press, 1987); and Gavin Wright, *Old South, New South: Revolutions in the Southern Economy since the Civil War* (Baton Rouge: Louisiana State University Press, 1996).

31. The Great Migration indicates that the South's boundaries were porous and many African Americans were eager to leave the South. Some studies of the migration include James N. Gregory, *The Southern Diaspora: How the Great Migrations of Black and White Southerners Transformed America* (Chapel Hill: University of North Carolina Press, 2005), and Isabel Wilkerson, *The Warmth of Other Suns: The Epic Story of America's Great Migration* (New York: Random House, 2010).

32. The catalog of Farm Security Administration photographs can be found online at the Library of Congress Web site, http://memory.loc.gov/ammem/fsahtml/fahome.html (accessed March 22, 2011). For background on the Farm Security

Administration, see Cara A. Finnegan, *Picturing Poverty: Print Culture and FSA Photographs* (Washington, D.C.: Smithsonian Institution Press, 2003).

33. For a discussion of Depression-era documentaries, see Stott, *Documentary Expression and Thirties America,* and Jeff Allred, *American Modernism and Depression Documentary* (New York: Oxford University Press, 2010).

34. Berkley Hudson and Ron Ostman, "A Desire to End These Things: An Analytical History of John L. Spivak's Photographic Portrayal of 1930s Georgia Chain Gangs," *Visual Communication Quarterly* 16 (October 2009): 200.

35. Stott, *Documentary Expression in Thirties America,* 33.

36. Barbie Zelizer, *Remembering to Forget: Holocaust Memory through the Camera's Eye* (Chicago: University of Chicago Press, 1998), 212.

37. Hudson and Ostman, "A Desire to End These Things," 204–6.

38. John L. Spivak, letter to William Stott, June 26, 1971, John L. Spivak Papers, Special Collections Research Center, Syracuse University Library.

39. Alex Lichtenstein, "Chain Gangs, Communism, and the 'Negro Question,'" 637.

40. Walter B. Rideout, *The Radical Novel in the United States, 1900–1954: Some Interrelations of Literature and Society* (Cambridge, Mass.: Harvard University Press, 1956), 12. Rideout categorizes Spivak's book as a radical novel "with some reservation" both because the Spivak used journalistic methods and because Spivak was not entirely sympathetic to communism (314).

41. Official prison statistics can be found online at the Web site of the Bureau of Justice Statistics, http://bjs.ojp.usdoj.gov/ (accessed April 6, 2011).

42. Media coverage of the strike was remarkably scant. For an example, see Sarah Wheaton, "Prisoners Strike in Georgia," *New York Times,* December 12, 2010. The strikers' list of demands can be found at the Web site of the Georgia Green Party, http://www.georgiagreenparty.org/blogs/bdixon/GA_InmatesStage HistoricOneDayPrisonStrikeToday (accessed April 6, 2011).

43. Heather Ann Thompson argues that northern prisons were also likely to commit human rights abuses in "Blinded by a 'Barbaric' South: Prison Horrors, Inmate Abuse, and the Ironic History of American Penal Reform," in *The Myth of Southern Exceptionalism,* ed. Matthew D. Lassiter and Joseph Crespino (New York: Oxford University Press, 2010), 74–98.

44. Michel Foucault, *Discipline and Punish: The Birth of the Prison,* trans. Alan Sheridan (New York: Vintage, 1995).

Frontispiece from the 1932 edition of *Georgia Nigger*.

PREFACE

To have placed the scene of action of "Georgia Nigger" in some specific county would manifestly have been unfair since it would have singled it out for national opprobrium when it is no worse than many others in the state or in other southern states; and to have presented a collection of factual, individual cases would have centered attention upon them and have left the many thousands of others as unknown as before.

Excellent studies in this field have been published by sociologists and penologists but these are too little known. I thought it wise to tell the story of David's efforts to escape from a monstrous system, in the guise of fiction. But though all characters in Georgia Nigger are fictitious some of the scenes described are so utterly incredible that I feel an appendix of pictures and documents are necessary in this particular work. The pictures I took personally in various camps and the documents are but a few of the many gathering dust in the State Capitol in Atlanta.

Georgia does not stand alone as a state lost to fundamental justice and humanity. It was chosen because it is fairly representative of the Carolinas, Florida, Alabama—the whole far-flung Black Belt. Nor is the whole south as pictured here. There are many counties where conditions are infinitely better, and too many counties where they are infinitely worse.

I do not believe that the overwhelming proportion of intelligent and humane citizens of the south approves these conditions. In those representative southerners, white and black, with whom I discussed my investigations and showed the pictures and documents, I found a sense of startled horror and a desire to end these things.

To those who are vaguely familiar with the lives in Georgia Nigger from the shocking cases which reach the press from time to time, and who may think I deliberately chose sensational and extreme instances for David to see and hear and pass through, I make assurances that I have earnestly avoided that, not only because it would not have been a representative picture but because the extreme cases are unbelievable.

To those, colored and white, who helped me with introductions which opened the doors of planter and cropper, peon and convict camp stockade, much gratitude is due.

J.L.S.

This preface was titled "Postscript" in the original edition.

GEORGIA NIGGER

To Mabel

I

TWO lanterns hung from the wooden cross driven deep in the red soil of the convict camp stockade. They threw a pale, yellow light over the ground and the steel cage on wheels so like a huge circus wagon in which ferocious feasts of the jungle are penned. The guard, staring absently at the sky, sat in an old chair tilted against the mess hall shack.

It is difficult to sleep when it is your last night on the chain gang and David peered through the latticed iron bars at the cross with its smoking lamps. There were thirteen men in the cage with him—nine negroes and five whites—sprawled on thin mattresses covering the iron bunks ranging the length of the cage on either side in three three-decker tiers. The six nearest the solid steel door were reserved

1

for whites. The fourteen men were naked to the waist. Their exposed bodies shone with sweat even in the semi-darkness.

"You kin take a bath in de ribber to-morrow," a voice from an adjoining bunk whispered enviously.

David did not answer. To bathe in a river, and a haunting devil always with him—that was Caleb's life. The toothless old convict, with a skin dried and withered by Georgia suns, had long since lost what little wit he had been born with and now spent his waking hours arguing with evil spirits and reliving the day when he had bathed in a river.

A mosquito lit on the boy's neck and he slapped at it casually. Flies hummed in the cage. Flies and mosquitoes were always entering through holes in the screen covering the bars and buzzing desperately to get out again. They were worse than the vermin you scratched at incessantly.

The guard, too, slapped at his ankles and arms and face. Somehow it helped you when you could not sleep, to know that the flies and mosquitoes annoyed him, too.

The mountainous mass of Sam Gates stretched on the bunk across the narrow aisle

2

from David turned slowly at the whisper and spat through cracked and swollen lips.

"You work out dis mawnin'," he said with difficulty, raising himself on an elbow.

"Yes, suh," the boy whispered.

"I wish I wukked out," Caleb announced eagerly.

The huge negro moved restlessly. His legs hurt. A steel spike resembling an ordinary pick extended ten inches in front and behind each ankle. The twenty-pound weight had rubbed against his feet until one leg had become infected. Shackle poison convicts called it. He had asked for a doctor and the guard's fist had crashed against his mouth. That had been yesterday and he had not complained again though the throbbing pain made it hard to work and impossible to sleep.

Everyone was afraid of this strapping prisoner doing life for murder. Sam Gates had killed a man on the farm where he had worked—broke the man's neck with his two hands. From the day two months ago when, chained hand and foot, he had been delivered to the Ochlockonee county camp at Snake Fork, he had terrified them. In his sullen eyes and powerful body was the tremendous,

3

quiet power of the primitive savage. Sam
Gates was a killer. Even the guards who tried
to break him and failed only hated and feared
him the more.

" How long you did, boy? " he asked.

" Six months."

" Six months! Dat ain' nothin'. I bin in
camps fo' five year an' I got a lot mo' tuh do
befo' dey takes dese offen me."

He raised the swollen foot in explanation
and let it down easily on the torn mattress.

"Yes, suh," said David respectfully.

" Five year," Sam repeated. " Five year,
an' a lot mo' tuh do—onless I kills dat boss-
man an' die out."

A prisoner, scratching himself drowsily,
raised his head.

" Gittin' up," he called.

The sleeping men tossed restlessly, disturbed by the cry.

" Git up," the guard shouted.

The convict's bare feet thudded on the floor.
The sharp clang of iron against iron drowned
the hum of the insects as the chains riveted
around his ankles struck the rim of his bunk.

He stumbled to a stool covered with wet
newspapers.

4

Under it was a zinc tub and the smell of its contents drew flies and mosquitoes nightly to feed in it. In the stifling heat the stench mingled with the stagnant odor of the nearby swamps and hung heavy over the cage. Sometimes a breath of hot wind shifted the pall rising from the tub. Then, for a beneficent moment, the air was filled with the south that was not of a convict camp and the prisoners breathed the sweet scent of rose and jasmine and rich magnolia growing luxuriously in the warden's yard.

" Gittin' back," called the convict standing motionless beside the stool.

" Git back," returned the guard.

The lean, leathery face of the man watching them was distinct in the light from the cross. The sleeves of his blue denim shirt were rolled to the elbows and the collar was open at the throat.

This was Charlie Counts' fourth year as guard. As illiterate as his parents he had grown up in the county like a weed in rich soil. Before his seventh birthday he had tasted the back-breaking toil of picking cotton under a broiling sun. As far back as he could remember he had always worked hard from dawn to dark. Somewhere in the years before he reached manhood he learned to write his name in a laborious scrawl.

There is little to be earned guarding the chained creatures who lay Georgia's roads but carrying a shotgun and leaning lazily against a shady tree is easier than sweating in the fields or breathing dust in a cotton gin, so Charlie Counts became a guard.

During his hours on duty he was lord and master. And though even poverty stricken Crackers look down upon a guard, the sense of power in having men under him soothed the harassing struggle to house and feed and clothe a wife and brood of ragged children on the dollar and twenty-five cents a day the county paid him.

To David Charlie Counts had not been harsh. The boy was a misdemeanor convict, born and raised in Ochlockonee county. Even the chains of captivity had been spared him during the past months. And now, within a few hours, he would be away from the clank of chains and the stink of the cage. He would be a freed man again.

There was work to be done at home. With these cloudless skies and tropic sun it would

6

be an early season. The speckled bolls of cotton were cracking open and dotting the fields with heads as white as his mother's counterpane; cotton to be picked under a friendly sky, with the black, shiny faces of his mother and father near and the dry drone of field insects for music while he and Henrietta followed the furrows and stuffed the sacks hanging from their shoulders. Henrietta would be joyous at her brother's return and little Zebulon, scampering barefooted in patched overalls, would do a jig in sheer delight.

David wondered as he had wondered so often in the long months on the chain gang whether it had been wise to reject Mr. Jim Deering's offer to pay the twenty-five dollar fine as an advance on a thirty-dollar a month job on the Deering plantation. There were ugly rumors about the white man. Those for whom he advanced fines somehow never quite succeeded in working them off. Sometimes they were never heard of again after they went to work for him.

It was Mr. Jim Deering whenever the boy thought of him. Mr. Jim Deering was a power, an important figure in county politics, a wealthy man with three or four thousand acres of cotton and corn, pecan groves and peanut farms. He was a director in the Southern Cotton Bank where the whites kept their money, and lived in a big house in a remote end of Ochlockonee county.

But the boy's father had advised against the planter's offer.

" I ain' specially keen 'bout hit," he had said. " Dey's bringin' yo' up tuh-morrer 'n' de co't o' ginral ju'sdiction ain' s'posed tuh set fo' t'ree months yet."

To the old man wise in the ways of the white man's south the haste was an ominous sign. He had heard of other negroes whom Mr. Deering had befriended. There were said to be men working for him whose fines he had advanced years ago, men never seen even on a Saturday evening in town. Mr. Deering always said the eighteen miles to the county seat at Live Oak was too long for the tired help.

A few of the planter's trusted men did come to town once in a while. He brought them in his Ford and when these found a bottle of white mule they sometimes whispered tales black men do not repeat too often even among themselves.

8

In that magic hour before the dawn when the heat of the night glides into the grateful coolness that follows fever, the fourteen caged men breathe more easily. Some turn restlessly and when you turn the sweat from your half naked body leaves a damp clot on the torn mattress. A rooster wandering from the warden's yard crows lustily. When you cannot sleep you hear him each morning. It presages your awakening.

The vast hulk of Sam Gates stirs. He bends his head over the edge of the bunk and spits through his cracked lips upon the floor.

Charlie Counts had called the cook and his helper from the dark shack in a corner of the stockade where the trusties slept. The weather-beaten clapboards that formed the kitchen were illuminated by a lamp suspended from a beam in the center. You could see them moving about, preparing breakfast for the convict crew, their shadows flying across the dusty window panes like gigantic bats.

With creaks that shrieked their message the rusty iron door of the cage turned on its hinges.

" Come an' git it! " the guard called loudly.

Dark shadows drop to the two-foot space between the tiers of bunks. Chains strike the iron floor with loud clanks and scrape over it with harsh rasps. In the half darkness they bump into each other and curse in undertones.

"Fo' Christ's sake!" a convict exclaims as his bare feet step into a puddle of spit.

"Watch yo' step!" another cries as a steel spike stabs his leg.

And above the noise Charlie Counts' voice rises louder:

"Come an' git it! Come an' git it! Reck'n you got all day!"

Grumbling sullenly the half naked men stumble down the four worn, wooden steps of the cage and pause on the cool, hard clay to scratch and pull on their striped coats. Some put on shoes through which their toes protrude.

A well three hundred yards from the barbed wire fence supplies water to the camp but the trusties are too busy preparing and serving breakfast to trouble about water for convicts. And when you sweat in a stinking cesspool all night you are too tired to pump water to wash your face and hands even if you are given per-

10

mission to go for it yourself. It does not matter anyway. You soon forget that you want to be clean when you dig dirt all day and sleep in it all night.

The dingy mess hall is lit by another kerosene lamp hanging from a beam and its yellow light glints off the six greasy, wooden benches at the greasier tables on each side of the hall. The place reeks with the hot smell of soap and coffee. A swarm of flies buzz angrily. They rise from tables and benches, from the floor and the walls and the ceiling. They circle about noisily and strike against you in their efforts to reach the open door.

White convicts sit at the tables to the left and the blacks at the right.

There is little talk. You gulp the unsavory coffee from a tin cup and with a tin spoon scoop mouthfuls of flour gravy, bits of salt pork and grits that is your portion before being led to the day's work.

The guard leans easily against the wooden cross, watching you.

Convicts finished their breakfast and left the mess hall, waiting for the truck that would take them to work. Caleb followed David out of the hall, stuffing a mouthful of the chewing tobacco the county rations each prisoner every week.

"Doan you come back yere, David," he grinned cheerfully.

The boy smiled.

"Doan you come back yere," the old man repeated earnestly, spitting a mouthful of tobacco juice.

"I'll sho try not tuh," David said simply.

"You won' jes' ez long ez you won' let de debbil git inter you 'n' ruination yo' soul lak he done did wid me."

Sam Gates approached, walking awkwardly, his shoulders hunched as though to ward a blow.

On the day a convict goes home those who remain crowd about to wish him well and the guard watched tolerantly the small group gathering about David.

"Yes, suh, Caleb," Sam Gates said good-naturedly, "I reck'n David kin git hisse'f a bath in a ribber now."

The old man's shoulders drooped.

"I had a bath in a ribber once," he began eagerly, scratching himself in excitement. "We wuz wukkin' a road down near de Flint an' de road, he tu'ned right aroun' f'um de

12

swamps an' run a-tween de ribber an' de swamps, an' it wuz hot. Yes, suh, dat wuz a hot day sho an' de boss-man, he says we kin bathe in de ribber——"

"Hey, you—Caleb an' Wesley," Charlie Counts interrupted. "Y'all'd better wash that pan."

The two convicts carried the tub under the cage to the swamp beyond the stockade to dump the night's contents.

A white trusty lit two pine torches that sputtered and crackled. He gave one to the guard and holding the flares high they took their places at the stockade gate, their shadows wavering over the ground.

The headlights of the work truck appeared and with a great sound of brakes halted at the entrance. The driver and the day guard got out and sat on the running board.

"Cap'n up yet?" they asked.

"There he is comin' yonder," Charlie Counts said.

Ray Alton moved loosely across the wide lawn separating his rambling house from the stockade. Tall and thin he seemed to be a bony framework covered by wrinkled trousers and a soiled, white shirt open at the throat.

"Line up!" the guards called.

The convicts formed an irregular line.

"Come by me!" the warden ordered sharply.

Each convict called his name as he passed through the gate and clambered on the truck. When the boy's turn came he called:

"David Jackson."

"You work out this mawnin', eh, Dave?" Alton asked good-naturedly.

"Yes, suh, Cap'n," he replied eagerly.

"Step out."

"Keep yo' eyes open fo' de debbil doan git in you," Caleb admonished as he passed.

"Oh, he'll be a good nigger now, Caleb," the warden smiled. "The devil ain't specially keen on him I reck'n, eh, Dave?"

The loaded truck thundered down the road. The flares were extinguished.

"Well, it's yore day, ain't it, Dave?" Alton remarked pleasantly.

"Yes, suh, Cap'n." The boy's white teeth could be seen in the expansive smile.

"Didn't have much o' clothes when you come here, did you?" The warden stared at David's unchained feet and the striped convict suit. "But you'll git some now."

14

The eight dollar outfit the state insists the county give you when your time is up was brought from the commissary: a pair of brogans two sizes too large, overalls, a jacket and a cap. It is supposed to have cost eight dollars but you could buy it in any town store for much less.

The boy stripped the convict suit and donned the county's gift. The light from the lanterns on the cross grew sickly. The deep purple of the southern sky turned wan in the east. The lamps were removed from the rusty nails and extinguished. The cross was bare and forlorn in the cold, morning light.

The warden brought his Ford from the blacksmith's barn.

" I'll take you home myself," he announced as he pulled up at the gate. " I have to go to town anyway."

He opened the door of the battered old car.

" Get in, boy," he invited. " You're a freed man now."

II

SEVEN miles from Snake Fork lay Shay
Pearson's sixteen hundred acres. Here,
was the first of the sagging shacks where his
croppers lived, a rude and dilapidated structure blistered by summer heat and swept by
years of wind and rain; and there, behind the
luxuriant branches of those towering live oaks,
peeked the dark, unpainted boards of another
cabin, with the morning sun on its roof. In
the fields deep in rich rows of cotton, croppers
worked their one-horse farms apportioned in
return for half their products, stuffing the
fruit of their year's labor into sacks hanging
from their shoulders.

Half way across his sprawling lands was the
planter's home, an oasis of opulence in a world
of ruined and decaying clapboards. Forty

16

thousand dollars that house cost and it compared with Jim Deering's, lost in his acreage at the other end of the county. Few ever saw the Deering mansion but Shay built his facing the main road so that anyone could see what a Cracker can do when he has ambition.

"I knew Mr. Pearson when he didn't even have a pair o' shoes for the winter," said the warden.

"Yes, suh," said David.

The Jacksons were Pearson niggers and David knew the story of the white man's rise. From the hopeless background of poor trash parents scraping a precarious subsistence from a two-horse farm he had become the second largest planter in Ochlockonee county. When his parents died and his brothers deserted the place for the city's opportunities, he was left alone to squeeze a living from the soil. He began with Isaiah Cleveland who owned an adjoining thirty-acre tract. Old Isaiah was a nigger so the aggressive young Cracker ploughed twenty feet over the balk into his neighbor's land. In three years Shay had so encroached on the property that Cleveland went to law about it only to learn that his title was questionable and that he owed his attorney one hundred and fifty dollars. The lawyer accepted a note secured by the property for the debt and Pearson bought it with money borrowed from the Southern Cotton Bank. In the fullness of time, after a season of rain and another of cheap cotton, old Isaiah's farm was knocked down to the white planter who permitted him and his family to work their old land as croppers. By loans and similar transactions Shay had acquired farm after farm and now ruled his lands and the thirty-two families on them, like a medieval lord.

A sow and two pigs wandered out of a side road and stood rooting in a ditch by the highway. A flock of buzzards, feeding on the carcass of a pig killed by a passing motorist, took wing at the car's approach and swarmed to the dead limbs of a tree to eye them owlishly.

" Won't be much left o' that there pig by the time I gits back," the warden commented amiably.

" No, suh. Reck'n not," the boy agreed, glancing back to the buzzards returning to the feast.

" I ain't never seed such smellers as them buzzards have. I once saw a pig run down like that there one was an' there wasn't a buz-

18

zard around an' a couple o' hours later when I passed by, them bones was picked clean. Picked clean they was."

He paused and added thoughtfully:

"Them buzzards has sho got wonderful smellers."

At a turn in the road David saw the familiar live oak rising before his home like a lonely sentinel, its wide-spread branches shading the roof of the rickety porch. The cabin rested on three brick stilts and an upright log of hickory.

"Well, I reck'n here's where you git out," the warden smiled. He pulled up at the deep wagon ruts of the narrow path lined with broom weeds that led to the house. "Good luck now, an' don't you go to gittin' into no mo' trouble!"

His parents and sister were probably at the far end of the field for only Zebulon, not yet old enough to work, was visible. The five-year-old boy was trying to ride a pig and at David's loud shout, fell off with excited squeals of glee.

There was an air of peace and tranquillity here: the sun on the white rows, that butterfly dipping over the heavy stalks, the noises of the field—even the pig grunting under the house added to the restfulness. That pig always rooted there, right under that crack in the floor where water from the drinking bucket dripped to the cool ground underneath. Bright red geraniums in rusty tin cans and broken earthenware ranged the porch and gave the drab boards an air of cheerfulness and color. The three rooms were spotless. The large cooking stove, with its pots and pans scrubbed shiny, was in the kitchen as when he had left. Nothing seemed changed and there was comfort in that knowledge.

He found a large cake of soap, a towel and a pair of old overalls. Zebulon watched curiously while he poured water into the large zinc tub his mother used for washing clothes.

" Gottuh git rid o' de lice an' crabs," David explained cheerfully. " You wouldn't want 'em crawlin' all over you, would you now? "

" No, suh! " the boy exclaimed with certainty. " Louise'd jes' smack hell outer me if I done got lousy! "

When the new clothes were left soaking in lye water to rid them of any vermin he might have brought from Snake Fork and his own body washed, David swung a cotton sack over a shoulder and with his little brother chatter-

20

ing at his side, went to the fields. He was needed there, and besides, Shay Pearson's overseer knew that he would be a freed man this day and the planter would be angry if Dee Jackson did not put his boy to work immediately when there was such a big early crop. Dee's monthly credit of twelve dollars included David's needs, and the boy was considered as much a Pearson nigger as his father.

Henrietta, a spindly-legged but comely girl of fourteen, dropped her half-filled bag and rushed to greet him. His mother, her hands pressing against the small of her back, straightened up and beamed happily. Dee stretched his long, angular form and carefully depositing his sack on the ground, smiled broadly. His mother hugged the boy, the tears filling her eyes.

" Here, here, Son! " his father protested affectionately. " You leab Louise alone! "

" Git away, you fool nigger! " she chided, pressing the boy closer. " Son, I'm sho happy you is back! "

" Blessin's on de Lawd," said Dee reverently.

They plucked the fluffy cotton from the wide-open bolls, Henrietta following a furrow beside her brother, laughing or exclaiming sympathetically at his stories of the chain gang. Zebulon scampered about, indifferent to the burning soil under his bare feet. Field insects hummed their dry songs and the heat waves quivered over the baking rows.

The gangling form of Shay Pearson's overseer, his long legs draped about a mule, came towards them.

"See you're back, Dave," the white man smiled pleasantly.

"Yes, suh. Jes' in time fo' work."

"Yeah. I reck'n Dee needs a li'l he'p. I'll tell Mr. Pearson you're back."

Dee approached hastily, wiping the sweat from his face with a sleeve.

"Sho glad tuh hab'm back," he said. "Fine picker, dat boy."

"Yeah. Good nigger," the overseer agreed, squirting a mouthful of tobacco juice.

With a careless nod he continued on to the next farm, his round shoulders drooping listlessly.

2

Dee Jackson could never see a mule without sad memories, for upon a mule and the

22

good Lord he had based a lifelong hope, had ploughed singing to a vision of freedom, and both had failed him. For years he had saved for that mule and a plough. With these and a little seed it was possible to rent a tract of ground and pay the owner one-fourth of the crop for the use of his land, and with a season or two of good crops and high prices, there would be money enough to make a down payment on a few acres. There were niggers in Ochlockonee county who had gone from tenant farming to independence.

The day he put his mark to an agreement with Shay Pearson for the use of twenty acres, and the mule and second-hand plough were paid for, was one of rejoicing. The mule was not as young and healthy as Dee would have liked but he was the best they could afford. Louise patched their clothes by the kerosene lamp and they did with little store food that winter for so much depended upon finishing the season clear of debt.

Those were feverish days at planting time when the winter vanished in the mellow warmth of spring. When perfect stands of cotton made the long rows a vivid green, Dee ploughed the middles again to make the beds

23

soft and with anxious care they thinned the luxuriant growths with appraising eyes. Then the blossoms appeared, flowering like good omens. The green bolls speckled, and under the burning July sun, cracked open with the smiling promise of money for their own farm. There would be almost a bale to the acre they told themselves happily.

But on the very day they went out for the first picking, it rained.

Fleecy clouds appeared in a suddenly overcast sky. Dee's face grew haggard and he clasped his hands together as in prayer. Louise looked up with a frightened air as though seeking help from the angry heavens. No one moved. And then it rained.

It seemed to them that the rain beat the fields with furious gusts of hate. Dee sank to the furrow as though the rain hammering his cotton to the ground had hammered him down, too.

And as suddenly as it had begun, the sky cleared and the sun shone hot again.

He did not stir. Louise touched him gently.

" Git up offen dat groun', Dee," she urged. " Ain' no sense carryin' on dat way."

" Oh, my good Lawd," he said dazedly.

24

The cotton had been whipped to the ground or hung dejectedly, their whiteness stained brown from the wet leaves. The crop was ruined. They would be lucky to get a third of what it would have brought.

"Dey'll be mo' pickin's," Louise said encouragingly.

There was only one consolation: the Lord who gave him his children, a helpful wife and the strength to work must have had a good reason to do that to him. Maybe he had been so busy ploughing and chopping and dreaming that the Lord thought he was becoming too independent and took that way to remind him that He was a jealous God, or perhaps some sin long since forgot was charged against him and He had demanded a settlement. The Lord kept mighty careful accounts.

Then, in the bleak winter days, the mule became sick.

Dee slept in the barn to attend his slightest need, but nothing seemed to help. That late December night when he returned to the cabin where the lamp with its smoking chimney threw his shadow across the room, his face told the story. Louise was waiting, wrapped in a blanket and huddled in the old rocker near the

25

stove. Twice she had been to the barn but when the mule stretched out, breathing in those painful, asthmatic gasps, Dee had sent her away.

"De Lawd knows His business," she said bravely.

"Yeah." He clasped and unclasped his hands, cracking the knuckles of his bony fingers.

"Sho He knows whut He's doin'." Her thick lips quivered. "He done gib you de money fo' tuh buy 'im an' now He takes 'im away."

The chair creaked over the loose boards in the floor.

"Sho. Lak chillun hit is. He done gib us seben an' tuk fo'."

"Dey didn't hab much tuh eat; dat's why dey tuk sick an' died," he said resentfully.

"Talkin' dat way ain' gontuh do you no good."

"You kin allus git chillun. But whey kin a nigger git a mule w'en he ain' got no money?"

Louise slid from the rocker to her knees.

"I ain' questionin' You none, Lawd," she prayed, "but did You hab tuh do dis tuh us? Ain' we done eb'ryt'ing You wants done?

An' now You frows us down lak dis. Caise maybe we didn't gib no money tuh de chu'ch. But Lawd, You knows we didn't hab no money."

Neighbors came with sympathy. Carts creaked to the Jackson cabin on the chilly evenings and tired blacks from surrounding farms sat before the fireplace and comforted them. Old Isaac Burr, who had ministered to the spiritual wants of Pearson niggers for a decade, came on Christmas night and told the story again of the Son of God Who came to spread the gospel of love and forgiveness; and as he talked a desperate hope awoke in Dee's breast.

"You reck'n de Lawd's too busy right now?" he asked earnestly.

"He's allus got plenty on His han's but His ears is wide open fo' anything His chillun ses tuh Him any time, anywhey in de hul worl'."

"Den lissen, Lawd!" Dee shouted, rising to his feet. "I ain' neber asked You fo' much but I'm askin' You now: gib me dat mule jes' fo' one mo' season, an' I'll neber ask You fo' nothin' no mo' in dis worl'. Neber. Sen' a clap o' Yo' thunder an' raise him f'um de daid.

You kin wuk all kinds o' miracles, Suh, an' dis is de las' chance I got. Lawd, doan You see dat I'll hab tuh go tuh Mist' Pearson if You doan gib me dat ol' mule back again? "

" Dey's a lot o' cullud folks wukkin' fo' Mist' Pearson," the preacher said mildly. " De Lawd knows His business an' if He wants you tuh be a croppah den He's got His own good reasons fo' hit. You kin bet on dat."

Dee took the lamp in a trembling hand and with old Isaac went to the mound back of the barn, hopeful that on this night of all nights, the miracle would happen: in a blinding flame of fire and a deafening clap of thunder the earth would be rent asunder and the mule would struggle to his feet ready for supper.

But there was no flame of fire nor clap of thunder. Only the lantern light and their shadows on the motionless mound, and a wind whistling.

Dee's head bowed.

" I reck'n dat settles hit, Lawd," he said dejectedly.

3

On the second day of the new year Dee got

off a neighbor's cart in Live Oak and went hesitantly to the Southern Cotton Bank, the red brick, one-story building across the square from the county court house and jail, and asked for Mr. Albert Graham, the president.

"Coming to deposit your savings, Dee?" the official greeted him jocularly.

"No, suh," he said nervously. "I done come tuh see you 'bout a li'l business matter."

"Sure. Always glad to talk business with you, Dee. Come right in and set yourself down."

"I'd lak tuh len' 'bout two hunnerd dollars, Mist' Graham," the old man stammered.

"That could be arranged, but have you any collateral?"

Dee looked puzzled.

"Something that will make sure the bank is repaid," Graham explained.

"Sho I'll pay hit back."

"I must have something as valuable in return," the banker said kindly. "Land—or a house ——"

"But I ain' got no lan'," Dee said helplessly, spreading his hands in a gesture of emptiness.

"You see, Dee," Graham pointed out regretfully, "we all know you and we know that if you have the money you will repay a loan. But now, suppose your crop is bad for a season or two—why, you'll hardly be able to pay the interest let alone the principal. Don't you see? And the bank must protect its depositors."

The Jacksons had been Ramsey niggers before the Civil War and Dee, depressed by the inevitableness of a cropper's contract, turned to Bayard Washington Ramsey as the last hope. The aristocratic white was known for his kindness, especially to descendants of his father's slaves. He lived a mile south of Live Oak in the mansion his father built before the lanky northern lawyer ruined the family's hundred and sixty thousand dollar investment in niggers, and too proud to enrich himself by Cracker tricks in dealing with blacks, had never increased the two hundred acre plantation left when the war ended and all creditors were paid.

The cook greeted Dee shrilly at the kitchen door of the Ramsey home.

" If hit ain' ol' Dee hisse'f! Whut you doin' heah?"

"I come tuh see Mist' Ramsey," he said with a worried air.

"Whut fo'?"

30

" I got tuh see 'im."

" Well, you jes' set right down heah an' I'll
go tell 'im."

When she returned she said, " Mist' Ramsey'll see you on de front po'ch. You go roun'
dey."

The tall, white-haired planter looked at him
questioningly.

" You're a long way from home, Dee," he
smiled. " What is it? "

" Mist' Ramsey, suh," the old man began,
twisting his hat nervously, " you 'bout de only
white man here'bouts we kin come to w'en
we is in trouble."

Ramsey looked gravely at him.

" An' I got mo'n a wagon load o' trouble
now."

" Yes, Dee."

" Mist' Ramsey, suh ——" The nervous
twisting of his hat became more pronounced.
" My mule done laid down an' died, suh."

The white man nodded sympathetically.

" I bin a hard wukkin' nigger all my bo'n
days," Dee continued, " an' I'm willin' tuh
wuk de res' o' my days some mo' but I ain' got
nothin' tuh wuk wid. No mule. No food. I
ain' got nothin'."

31

Ramsey pursed his lips and stared at his fields naked in the winter's day.

" I jes' was ober tuh de bank fo' tuh ask 'em tuh len' me two hunnerd dollars so's I kin git me a mule an' a li'l food tuh tide us ober till de nex' crop comes but Mist' Graham done said I'd hab tuh hab col—col ——"

" Collateral," Ramsey said quietly.

" Yes, suh. Collateral. But I ain' got no collateral. I ain' got nothin' ceptin' my two han's, an' my wife, an' David an' Henrietta."

" Yes, I know."

" An' I'll hab tuh sign wid Mist' Pearson if I cain' git no two hunnerd dollars an' if I goes tuh wuk fo' Mist' Pearson ——"

" Yes, I know," Ramsey repeated.

" So I done come tuh you, suh," Dee burst forth pleadingly. " I doan want tuh be Mist' Pearson's nigger. Me, an' Louise an' David an' Henrietta, we'll wuk fo' you 'n' pay you back, suh, if you'll len' hit tuh me."

Ramsey shook his head slowly.

" I can't, Dee. I'd like to help you but I haven't money enough to start saving all the nigras in the county. I have to take care of my own nigras. If I loan you two hundred dollars and another two hundred to some other
32

nigra caught in the Cracker buzz saw I should soon be in the same situation you are in."

Perspiration broke out in tiny beads on Dee's forehead.

" Yes, suh," he said. " Thankee, suh."

" You see, Dee," Ramsey added, putting a hand gently on the old man's shoulders, " I'm caught in their buzz saw, too."

" Yes, suh," said Dee.

4

Dee would have left the county but there was no place to go. There was not even a mule to pull the few sticks of furniture that were his household goods, nor food for a journey, and no matter where a penniless nigger went he would have to work for someone. In Ochlockonee county they knew him for a good nigger and would be more considerate than would strange whites in another county or another state, so two days later Dee Jackson put his cross to the usual cropper contract.

It provided that Pearson supply him with a mule, seed, and a monthly advance of twelve dollars between February and August inclusive, in return for half his crop after all advances and interest thereon were deducted.

The agreement particularly specified that should the "*said tenant fail to pay the advances made by the owner when due, the tenant agrees to surrender the possession of said premises, in which event the owner is hereby authorized to sell or dispose of all property thereon the tenant has any interest in*" and concluded with the ominous words "*and shall be so construed between the parties thereto, any law, usage or custom to the contrary notwithstanding.*"

Dee could not read but he knew what it contained. Others had signed cropper agreements and were charged eighteen percent interest on advances, and with the Pearson bookkeeping system, a nigger never got out of debt. And Dee knew also that the Georgia law provided that as long as he owed the planter one dollar he could not leave the Pearson farm without facing arrest and the chain gang for swindling.

So Dee Jackson became Shay Pearson's nigger.

34

III

SEVEN hundred and eighty pounds the Jacksons weighed in before the sun set behind the pines. Louise led the way home, her feet dragging along a furrow. Even the empty sack hanging from her shoulder seemed limp and exhausted.

David scratched himself tiredly. His mother turned at the sound.

"Didn't you scrub yo'se'f, Son?" she demanded. "You ain' gone an' brung no lice home, did you?"

"Sho I scrubbed myse'f. Scrubbed myse'f good. Dis scratchin's jes' a nachral habit, I reck'n."

"Better not bring no camp lice intuh my home," she said severely. "I got all I kin do tuh keep hit clean as 'tis. If dat house gits

35

lousy I'll mek you scrub hit f'um top tuh bottom, Lawd mek me stumble an' fall in sin if I doan!"

The southern night and the stillness around the cabin lost in the twenty acres, the kerosene lamp and its cheery light, the cream-colored dishes and heavy cups on the red-and-white, checkered table-cloth gave David a sense of peace and security. And in Dee and Louise was a deep thankfulness that the Lord had returned them their son.

After supper Zebulon was put to bed and the women washed the dishes in a large, tin pan while Dee and his son sat on the porch steps and smoked their corn-cob pipes.

" I hears dey's payin' a dollar an' a half a day in de cotton mills," Dee said slowly.

" Yeah. How you figger'n gittin' dey? "

" I got fo' dollars an' sixty cents. Made hit shootin' crap once in town," he added apologetically.

David did not answer.

" I started wid a quarter," Dee explained with a touch of pride, and then hastily, " but dat was a sin an' I ain' sinned sence. I ain' eben spent hit caise I got hit gambelin' but I figgered maybe some time I'd git a chance tuh

36

spend hit on somethin' de Lawd wouldn't mind."

"Yeah? On whut?"

"Well, I figgered maybe you'd lak tuh git outuh de county an' go tuh wuk in a mill town."

The boy peered at him suspiciously.

"Whut you want tuh git rid o' me fo'?" he asked. "Ain' you wantin' me roun' here no mo'?"

"Sho I want you roun' here, Son, but I figgered maybe dis county ain' no place fo' a young nigger. I b'longs tuh Mist' Shay an' fo' I knows hit Mist' Shay'll gib you twenty acres an' you'll b'long tuh him, too."

"Got tuh be somebody's nigger. An' Mist' Shay's as good as a lot o' dem an' maybe some better. If I takes yo' fo' dollars an' sixty cents some deputy'll pick me up fo' I gits outen de nex' county an' take my money away an' den sen' me tuh de chain gang fo' bein' a vagrant."

"I figgered maybe you could git tuh a mill town if you pays de bus fare," his father said hesitantly.

"Yeah. Dey was two niggers in camp who tried hit an' dey had mo'n fo' dollars. Dey was headin' fo' New Orleans an' dey headed right smack intuh de chain gang on de way. You cain' go no place now—not wid all dem fiel's an' ev'rybody wantin' husky niggers tuh pick'm."

" I figgered maybe you could do hit, Son," Dee said quietly.

" If I stays here an' minds my own bus'ness dey ain' nobody goin' tuh trouble me. I ain' fixin' tuh git uppity roun' here. I'll jes' mind my own bus'ness an' ten' tuh my wuk right here wid you. Dis place's plenty good fo' me."

" Hit's alright wid me, Son. I ain' schemin' tuh git rid o' you. I jes' figgered maybe you'd be a smart sight better off."

Louise and Henrietta joined them. The shaky boards creaked under Louise's weight.

" Gi' me some tuhbaccy," she said, striking the bowl of her pipe against her knee.

Dee gave her the can. She filled the bowl and struck a match.

" Dat trouble o' Preacher Isaac wid Mist' Shay's all patched up, I hears," she said with a pleased air. " Po' ol' man. He was jes' frettin' hisse'f sick Mist' Shay'd take his chu'ch away an' plant de groun' wid cotton."

38

"Yeah," Dee said thoughtfully. "Dat's whut he got messin' roun' wid things dat ain' his bus'ness."

2

Old Isaac Burr was a Pearson cropper who did his earthly work with eyes set heavenward and who lived for the hours when he preached God's word to his flock. He had never learned to read or write but he had heard the Bible read so often that he knew many verses and these he used for texts. Pearson niggers met in his cabin until the planter gave them a plot of ground on which to build a church and each year, after the crop was baled, donated a coat of paint for the building. There was not a cropper on his lands who was not proud of the church and its tall spire. And then old Isaac told his congregation, casually, in the course of a sermon, that black children do not have as good a chance for an education as white ones. The listeners accepted it as a truism and paid no further attention to it but the planter, when he passed the Burr farm, summoned him. The old man came, bowing and smiling.

"Preacher," Pearson began, "my niggers

roun' here are a pretty contented lot, ain't they?"

"Yas, suh," he smiled. "Dey sho is!"

The planter rubbed his chin reflectively.

"A preacher's job's to spread the gospel, ain't it? Every time I heard you, you talked fine."

"Thank you, suh. Thank you. I allus tries to gib 'em de Good Book's wuds de bes' I kin."

"That's jes' it. Why don't you jes' stick to your job an' git 'em in right with the Lord instead o' puttin' ideas into their heads that'll make trouble."

"Who? Me? Why, Mist' Pearson, I bin libin' here all my life an' I ain' bin one to make no trouble! Somebody's lyin' to you, suh."

"I was told you said something 'bout nigger children not gittin' as good a education as the whites."

The old man looked puzzled.

"I doan remember, suh," he said, "but maybe I did say dat. Lawd, Mist' Shay, dat ain' no lie. Eb'rybody knows hit."

"Yeah. Everybody knows it but there's no sense rubbin' it in. First thing you know all my niggers here'll start frettin' about it an'

40

askin' fo' a lot o' things the county can't afford. That would only git 'em in wrong. You wouldn't want nothin' like that to happen, would you now? "

"Lawd, no, suh!" the old man exclaimed, frightened. "Us niggers doan wan' no trouble! "

"Well, you probably didn't mean nothin' but remarks like that can start an awful lot o' misunderstandin'. Naturally, I figgered that if the church built on my land was used to start trouble amongst my niggers, well—nobody could expect me to give up valuable property to be used for that."

"No, suh," he agreed miserably.

"I reck'n it was jes' a accident an' it won't happen no mo'. I jes' figgered I'd mention it to you while I was passin' by."

"Yas, suh. I'se sho glad you did. I'll watch my wuds mo' keerful, suh."

3

"Niggers'll allus hab trouble," Dee said slowly, breaking the silence.

"Yeah," said Louise.

"White folks hab troubles, too," Dee said thoughtfully. "Eb'rybody's got trouble."

41

4

The unpainted wagon, with tufts of cotton clinging to cracks in the rough boards, joggled over the road to Preacher Isaac's church. Henrietta was gay with a yellow ribbon in her hair and Louise sat proud in her calico dress. But Dee, though dressed in his lone pair of black pants and blue, meeting-night shirt, was far from worldly thoughts. On this night he would sing and the Lord would hear him. There would be a clean feeling in his heart. He always felt like his spirit was washed clean after such an evening, clean as fresh cotton peeking through a cracking boll. There was comfort in knowing there is a God and a heaven beyond a world of cotton rows and nigger shacks.

A hen flapped its wings excitedly, to escape the wagon.

They heard thunderous voices raised in song before they saw the church with its friendly, lighted windows. There was a primitive yearning in the sound, a communion with God and the promise of a future where there is no work nor worry but only rest, and good things to eat, and angels playing harps and singing praises of the Lord; where the saved could

42

peek through holes in heaven's golden floor and see sinners sizzling on huge pine logs or picking cotton under a Georgia sun forever and forever, without even a drink of water for their cracked lips.

Four lanterns, suspended by twisted strands of wire from beams in the ceiling, threw grotesque shadows of the fifteen niggers already there when the Jacksons entered. Door and windows were wide open but the church reeked of perspiration. Insects hurled themselves at the lights or settled on the unfeeling bodies of the congregation sitting on long, moveable benches. There were croppers in overalls and in store suits bought in opulent days, women in bright dresses and barefooted youngsters; and facing them from the raised platform was old Isaac with the white shirt reserved for prayer meetings glaring on his bosom. His preacher's coat fell below his knees and even by lantern light it seemed to show an age-old mossiness, but it was his insignia as the shepherd of a flock and he would as soon have appeared naked before them as without it.

"Come in! Come right in, Brother Jackson!" he shouted.

He sang:

Sinnuh, whut you gonter do
W'en de debbil git you?

The congregation picked up the song:

Whut you gonter do
W'en de debbil git you!
Whut you gonter do
W'en de debbil git you!

"Lawd, I'm on my way!" Dee replied
lustily. The congregation roared:

Lawd, I'm on my way!

More Pearson niggers came. The loneliness of farms and the drabness of daily lives
were forgotten. As the head of each family
entered old Isaac shouted greetings between
the intoned words of a spiritual. Sweating
faces turned to him with abiding faith: an old
man, his hands wrinkled by a life of toil,
whose thick, flabby lips trembled as he sang;
a barefooted old woman, her face marked by
a century's lines, leaned forward eagerly. Her
thin, withered hands held a cold pipe. Stone

44

deaf, she did not hear a sound but her rheumy eyes were glued to the preacher.

Old Isaac was crying. Tears rolled down his cheeks and he wiped them with the palm of a hand.

"Yas, Lawd!" he cried. "Dey's yo' chillun—li'l black chillun!"

His white goatee quivered with emotion. The old, deaf woman nodded approvingly.

"Amen," she murmured.

He raised clenched fists high overhead. He was like an ancient prophet come among them.

"Doan y'all go to figgerin' dat all you gotter do is to start prayin' an' beggin' de Lawd to fo'gib you an' promisin' Him to be good w'en y'all's too ol' to be bad. De Lawd ain' nobody's fool! He got His eyes wide open all de time an' He's watchin' you—watchin' you pusson'ly! You cain' pull a pair o' loaded dice on Him. No, suh! You try dat an' y'all lose jes' as sho's my name's Isaac Burr! Y'all lose an' find yo'se'f sizzlin' in hell an' de debbil right ober you laughin' till his sides hu't, an' I sho won't blame him none!

"One o' dese days a angel tek a look down here an' say to de Lawd, 'Lawd, dose black

niggers down on de Pearson farm ain' payin'
no 'tention a-tall to whut yo' preacher's tellin'
'em. All dey wants is to fill dey bellies an' buy
some new clo'se an' shoot crap an' do a li'l
fornicatin'. Lawd, doan You reck'n we better sen' a li'l fire an' brimstone an' git finished
up wid 'em? Dey a bunch o' no good niggers
anyhow—jes' sinnin' an' fornicatin' all de
time!'

"But de Lawd's kind. Oh, my chillun, y'all
doan know how kind He is, blessed be His
name. He's got a heart bigger'n de hul' worl'
an' He'll say, 'Oh, le's gib 'em one mo'
chance. Dey ain' no use whippin' 'em now.
My Son was crucified wid nails through His
body jes' to sabe wuthless niggers lak dem.
Sho, le's gib 'em one mo' chance!'

"He's allus gibbin' you one mo' chance—
an' whut y'all doin' wid hit?"

His voice rose in a terrifying question. But
the emotion was too great for him and his
arms dropped to his sides with a helpless
gesture.

"Oh, my po' chillun—whut y'all doin' wid
yo' chance?" he asked brokenly.

A woman sobbed. An old man cried loudly,
"Lawd, O Lawd, fo'gib a ol' nigger fo' his
46

sins!" Dee's head bowed. Louise wiped a tear from her perspiring face.

"Boy, dat's preachin'!" a voice shouted enthusiastically.

"Yes, suh!" another cried.

"Gib hit tuh 'em, Preacher!" an old woman shouted hysterically. "Lawd, you ain' tol' 'em de half ob hit yet!"

5

It was in the early hours of the morning before the singing and shouting ended. In Dee's heart was a serene peace. He felt that he was in right with the Lord. Henrietta was asleep, tired by the emotional strain. David stared moodily at the star-lit fields.

The wagon creaked through the ruts.

"I sho feels a lot better," said Dee.

"He preached fine dis eb'nin'," his wife said admiringly.

A great contentment was over them.

IV

THE county seat nestling in sleepy indo-
lence on the hot Georgia plain for six
days of the week awoke on Saturday afternoon.
Wagons lumbered out of dusty, red highways,
the mules and horses wet with perspiration.
They were left on the outskirts of the town and
in side streets while an invading horde of
blacks swarmed to the center of the town: men
with sleeves rolled up and collars open, women
in their Sunday best, sweating profusely, chid-
ing and smacking their offspring. Niggers
within a ten mile radius were coming to town,
some to buy necessities or exchange produce
for clothes and flour, tobacco and kerosene;
but most just to wander about aimlessly or rest
in the shade of awnings over stores, glad to
escape the loneliness of their farms. The town
hall square, the street corners and the side-

48

walks were cluttered with them. There were seven or eight blacks to every white in Live Oak.

Dusty Fords and white farmers' wagons lined the paved square. Crackers in overalls, and their women in faded Mother Hubbards, rambled about as aimlessly as the blacks. Loud music blared from a radio store facing the county jail adjoining the town hall. A group collected before the loud speaker on the sidewalk. Two black children joined hands and hopped about joyously to the amusement of bystanders who laughed and clapped hands in tune with the dance.

The benches on the town hall lawn were occupied by whites. The blacks congregated on corners and in front of stores or sat on curbs puffing corn-cob pipes. Niggers did not walk on the lawn except to drink at the public pump from a tin dipper hanging under a sign " Colored." On the other side of the pump marked " White," ragged and barefooted white children splashed water over one another with loud shouts of glee.

As the sun set behind the one and two story buildings, bringing a measure of relief from the heat, a white man in a soiled shirt and wrinkled trousers, issued from a side street, his arms loaded with hymn books and a Bible. His fat jowls and protruding belly swayed with each step. The paunch almost hid a heavy, gold watch chain hanging from his belt. As he advanced upon the lawn a number of middle-aged and old men and women rose. His red face was damp with perspiration and he wiped it with a sleeve, smiled greetings, and distributed the hymn books.

The elders dragged little boys with pinched faces and barefooted little girls with long, thin hair drooping to their shoulders, to join in a semicircle under a stately live oak. There was meekness in the children's eyes and the grave expression of serious old age.

A crowd of whites gathered near the pump while the blacks watched from across the wide street.

The fat man waved the Bible.

"We will open with the hymn *Hold Out to the End*," he announced loudly. His voice was husky.

> *I bin prayin' in the valley so long,*
> *I ain't got tard yet.*
> *I bin prayin' in the valley so long,*
> *I ain't got tard yet.*

50

He kept time by waving the Bible. The veins in his neck showed blue against his red throat. The singing suffused his face with a deeper red. The scrawny old men and women followed in dismal discord. The children sang shrilly.

A popular tune crashed from the radio, almost drowning their voices.

The fat man paused for breath and again wiped his face with a sleeve.

> *Hold out, my Brother, hold out to the end,*
>   *I ain't got tard yet.*
> *Hold out, my Brother, hold out to the end,*
>   *I ain't got tard yet.*

The voice rose raucous and loud. The old women screeched, their eyes raised to heaven.

The crowd stared. The niggers across the street nodded and murmured, " Amen."

2

From the wide, granite slabs of the town hall steps Jim Deering and Sheriff Dan Nichols watched the niggers. There was power and force in the planter's tall, spare form. The nostrils of his aquiline nose distended slightly over thin lips. A large, felt hat shaded his gray eyes.

The sheriff's glance roamed to the stores facing the square.

"Reck'n they won't do much buyin' this ev'nin'," he remarked.

Deering glanced at his shiny, leather puttees.

"I've got seventy acres that haven't been picked," he said quietly. "Before we turn around it'll be time to work the peanut farms."

Nichols nodded sympathetically.

"These damn niggers don't want to work," Deering added.

A frown flashed across the sheriff's heavy face.

"I don't want to tell you how to run yo' business, Jim," he said hesitantly, "but I wouldn't jes' take 'em. Some o' these niggers git away an' do a lot o' talkin'. I haven't forgotten the hell raised over that last batch you took."

The planter's eyes moved restlessly over the streets.

"I don't intend to lose money just because niggers are too lazy to work," he said pointedly.

52

" Some o' these young bucks'll git into trouble befo' the ev'nin's over," the sheriff suggested.

" That's a likely-looking nigger," said Deering, nodding towards one crossing the street.

" That's a Clayton nigger," the sheriff protested quickly.

" I don't give a good God damn whose nigger he is."

Nichols shrugged his shoulders and turned to the open window of his office where Jess Pitkin, one of his deputies, sat with feet on the window sill surveying the visitors.

" Jess," he called, " I wish you'd keep an eye on Tom Mathers, Clayton's nigger. He's bin gittin' kind o' biggity lately an' may git into trouble."

The deputy spat a mouthful of tobacco juice, wiped his chin with the palm of a hand, and rose.

" I'm going over to the bank," Deering said abruptly. " I want at least four."

The sheriff nodded and wiped the sweat from his hat band.

3

In the years Jim Deering had been amassing

his wealth, few were known to have received wages from him even in seasons when crops brought high prices. He cheated his niggers so openly that they risked the anger of the law and ran away. Even whites who went to work for him fled.

There was difficulty with labor each year and each year at planting time the sheriff, placed in office by the politically influential landowner, picked up foot-loose niggers in the county who, rather than serve time on the chain gang for vagrancy, usually agreed to work off the fines the planter offered to pay. Two years ago, at a time when Deering's acres were blanketed with a stupendous crop, other farmers demanded their share of vagrants. He offered forty dollars a month but no Ochlockonee nigger would sign and in desperation he forced three blacks and one white into his car at the point of a pistol and took them to his farms. The white escaped and found his way to Atlanta and the resulting difficulty gave Dan Nichols trouble before it was smoothed over.

The county niggers feared Deering. There were rumors that he had armed guards to keep his workers from running away. The white man told of it in Atlanta but the planter explained that the function of the armed watch was to protect his property. A crazy nigger had once set fire to a barn and after that the patrol was established, he said.

4

The afternoon sun beat upon the creaking Jackson wagon. No neighbor was visible on the road to Live Oak; they were alone in a world of heat waves dancing on a deserted highway. The perspiration ran down Dee's face. Louise's polka dot dress clung damply to her body. Her neck glistened under a large, straw hat.

Saturday meant half a day's work and relaxation among people, streets and bright lights and store windows; an ice cream cone or a red lolly-pop for Zebulon, and boys who would jostle Henrietta's skinny body and send thrills of awakening sex through her, and for David, there was adventure when the sun set and black girls laughed invitingly in the half-lighted streets and alleys of Nigger Town.

Dee halted his mule in an open lot two blocks from the town hall square. Two young niggers standing beside a nearby wagon ogled Henrietta with glances that brought giggles from her.

"Doan you go tuh laughin' at dem niggers," Louise said irritably.

"Leab de chile be," Dee advised mildly. "Ain' you neber laughed w'en you was a fool gal?"

"I ain' neber laughed dat foolish!" She slapped the girl briskly. "Why, dat gal ain' ol' enough tuh know her own name an' here she's makin' eyes at 'em! A sin, dat's whut hit is!"

"You done a li'l sinnin' yo'se'f w'en you was a gal. Leab de chile be."

David jumped from the wagon with an angry frown and the two youngsters turned away.

"Dey's Mist' Deerin'," Dee said abruptly, nodding to the sun-baked street which the planter was crossing.

"He didn't come tuh buy no kerosene," Louise said under her breath.

"He neber do come tuh town on Sat'dee widout wantin' he'p on his farms. De sheriff'll be pickin' up some stray niggers dis eb'nin' fo' sho."

56

Louise turned sharply to David:

"You keep outuh mischief, d'you hear? I doan wan' you tuh go gittin' intuh no trouble an' git carried tuh de chain gang again."

"He'll be alright," Dee said slowly, "but dey ain' no sense gittin' intuh no messes."

5

Four blocks north of the square was the first of the squalid buildings of Nigger Town. It sagged on an unpaved street across from the home of a poor white who did odd jobs in Live Oak. Nigger Town wound in a semi-circle around the county seat and petered out in little clearings of cabbages and tomatoes or weed-covered fields. Winding, dusty lanes were its streets and flies buzzed about the cakes of horse dung that dotted them.

The paint on Nigger Town homes had long since worn off but their ugliness was hidden by rambler roses and leafy vines that twined over the trellised porches and clambered up the walls. Here, on lazy Saturday afternoons, old men and women sat drowsily on the stoops, smoking their pipes and staring somnolently at the children playing on the red streets.

In Mockingbird Alley was the clean little

house owned by Magnolia Holland. Each year it was given a coat of paint and when spring and summer came the verandah was almost hidden by honeysuckle vines. Its windows were draped with spotless curtains and at night heavy blinds were drawn. It had the air of a deserted place by day but when the town lights showed bright in the distance it became alive. Laughter mingled with soft tunes from a radio and niggers came to ring the door-bell.

Near her house was a lunch room with an orange and yellow sign " Eats." The restaurant's lone window was opaque with the dirt and dust of weeks and on Saturday nights niggers with a little money gathered under the yellow light struggling through to the sidewalk and shot crap.

These were Live Oak's oases for visiting blacks and though fights often started there, the sheriff closed his eyes. Niggers were needed for the county's public work and the law could always find there a supply of misdemeanor offenders.

6

Once a young wench had hailed David

softly from a porch and he always passed the house when in town but the call was never repeated. Only from dark alleys still warm with the day's heat, white men whispered furtively as he passed:

"Hey, nigger, want a drink?"

David knew that he who had a dime stepped into the alley and passed it quickly to an outstretched hand. A bottle was tendered and tilted upward. There were many Crackers peddling white mule made on lonely farms and brought to town expressly for the Saturday visitors.

In the hazy light from the lunch room seven niggers eagerly watched Fate roll two dotted cubes. Dimes and quarters lay on the sidewalk. David stopped to peer enviously at a youth rubbing the dice between his palms.

"One dollar I makes dat six," the player called. "Come on, gambelers, whey's yo' money?"

"Half a dollar sez you gwine frow a seben," a voice announced.

The clang of silver on the sidewalk rang its sharp challenge.

"I got a quarter of hit," another said.

"Fifteen cents sez yo's clean outer yo' haid!"

"Ten cents mo'! One dime mo'! Whassa matter? Ain' y'all got no money? Wha' you doin' in dis heah crap game? Doan y'all call yo'se'f gambelers! Gambelers, huh! Jes' a lot o' cheap niggers, dat's all you is!"

"Two dollars sez you is a cheap nigger yo'se'f," a deep voice said coldly.

A huge black threw two dollar bills on the pile of change.

"Go on, mister," he urged, "dey's two dollars. Cover hit, an' hush yo' big mouf!"

The thrower paused in fondling the dice.

"I'm bettin', cullud man, an' I'm bettin' one dollar. Hit's my frow."

"All you frow is a lot o' hot air," the challenger said contemptuously, and picked up the bills.

Someone laughed nervously. Another called irritably:

"Come on, do yo' singin' in chu'ch. Frow de dice or pass 'em tuh somebody as will frow 'em! Dis ain' no prayer meetin'. Frow 'em or pass 'em!"

The holder of the dice blew into his palms.

"Mudder Mary," he prayed, "show dese

60

niggers how you an' li'l Jesus pair up on t'rees!"

The cubes flashed out of his hands. A five and a deuce lay uppermost.

"Haw!" the deep voice exclaimed. "Try God hisse'f nex' time!"

"You jes' shoot yo' mouf off too damn much, nigger," the loser growled.

"Maybe you'd lak tuh close hit?"

A steel blade glinted in the yellow light. The burly nigger grunted and clutched at his neck. The assailant dropped the knife and fled. Someone scooped up the money and ran. Only the knife was left by the time the restaurant proprietor and his two customers rushed out.

David instinctively turned to the lighted streets, hoping to lose himself in the crowds. Dark forms scurried by. A strong hand grasped the boy's arm, and a voice demanded:

"Whut's yo' hurry, nigger?"

David lunged to break the hold and was slapped across the mouth.

"Stay still," the voice warned, "or I'll bust yo' haid!"

"I didn't do nothin'," he protested frantically.

61

Another deputy with a frightened nigger in tow came up.

"Here," he panted, "hold this one!"

David rubbed his bruised lips. The sheriff and Jess Pitkin appeared, each with a prisoner.

"I got the knife," Nichols said triumphantly. "How many we got?"

"Four, an' Buck's after another."

"Sheriff," pleaded one of the prisoners, "I was walkin' down de street an' doan know nothin' a-tall 'bout all dis! What'd he want to 'rest me fo'?"

"Hush!" Nichols ordered harshly, raising a threatening hand.

The prisoners were marched to a street light.

"Oh," said the sheriff, "yo're that Clayton nigger that's bin gittin' biggity ev'ry time you come to town!"

"Sheriff," the boy said earnestly, "I was walkin' down de street——"

"An' you," Nichols turned to David, "yo're the nigger that's jes' back from the chain gang, huh?"

"Yes, suh," said David, "but I doan know whut hit's all about, suh. I was watchin' de

62

game an' w'en de fight started I jes' run lak ev'rybody else ——"

" You didn't do the cuttin', did you? " the sheriff demanded.

" No, suh! Lawd, no, suh! "

" Then what did you run away fo'? "

" I didn't want tuh git in no trouble ——"

" Bad nigger," the sheriff interrupted with a shake of his head. " Like as not did the cuttin'."

" Sheriff, I tells you I didn't do nothin'! "

" He's a Pearson nigger," Jess Pitkin remarked casually.

" Sheriff, I swears wid my han' on de Bible I ain' hu't nobody. Nobody! I was jes' watchin' de game ——"

Reports of the stabbing spread. From a man knifed they grew to a nigger killed, two wounded and eight arrested. A crowd gathered on the jail steps. Those arrested were being booked and everyone was anxious to learn the identity of the dead man, the injured and the prisoners. After a fruitless search for David Dee left Henrietta and Zebulon with Louise and, hat in hand, pushed his way up the stairs to the deputy guarding the screened outer door.

" Kin I go in, suh? " he pleaded.

The deputy carefully selected a spot on the lawn and spat upon it.

" Nobody 'lowed in," he said.

Dee waited with the others until Dan Nichols appeared. The sheriff was immediately besieged with questions.

" Who bin kilt, suh? " an old woman asked tearfully.

" Nobody, aunty," he assured her pleasantly. " Jes' a li'l cuttin' in a crap game. Ain' nobody bin killed."

There was a sigh of relief at the news. The sheriff bit a chew from a plug of tobacco and continued:

" Five o' the nigras in the fight's bin arrested an' are now in there. Nothin' to worry about."

" Who's bin arrested? " Dee asked fearfully.

Nichols noticed him for the first time and frowned.

" Yo're Dee Jackson, ain't you? " he asked.

" Yes, suh," Dee said.

" That boy o' yourn's allus gittin' into trouble." The sheriff shook his head disapprovingly.

" Whut he do, suh? "

64

Other voices queried:

" Who else bin arrested? "

" Kin I see David? " Dee pleaded.

" No. Can't nobody see anybody jes' now."

" Mist' Nichols," Dee persisted, " cain' you tell me, please, suh, whut he's charged wid? "

" Gamblin', fightin' an' resistin' the law," the sheriff said curtly. " He's a bad nigger, that boy o' yourn, Dee! "

V

THE wheels crunched in the road ruts. Dee's shoulders swayed with each motion as though he were part of the flat board on which he sat, part of the one-horse wagon. The reins dangled listlessly in his hands.

" I jes' felt hit in my bones dey'd be trouble w'en I seen Mist' Deerin'," Louise said.

A wagon ahead stopped before a cabin etched on a ghostly field of cotton.

" Dey was fifty husky niggers in town," Louise said again.` " Why did dey have tuh 'res' David? "

A loose wheel rattled. Zebulon kicked a board restlessly in his sleep.

" Doan jes' set dey lak you's daid! " she exclaimed irritably. " Ain' you got nothin' tuh say! "

66

" Nothin'," he said slowly.

" Why did dey have tuh 'res' David? " she repeated bitterly.

" Mist' Deerin' has a lot o' cotton he wants picked."

Tears rolled down her cheeks. She shook her head dejectedly.

" Doan tek on lak dat," Dee said.

" An' me a chu'ch member. Why did de good Lawd, bless His name, amen, have tuh do dis tuh me? "

" De Lawd didn't do hit. Dey'd a-carried David off eben if dey hadn't bin no fight." His voice trembled slightly.

" Jes' de meanes' white man eber was bo'n."

" Yeah."

" I hope he bu'ns in hell fo'eber an' eber."

" Dat'd sho he'p David now. Why doan you hush? "

" I cain', Dee," she cried pitifully. " I'm all broke up inside an' I'm scairt dey'll sen' him away again."

" No, I reck'n not. You cain' pick cotton on de roads."

" But David b'longs tuh us. He wuks fo' us an' fo' Mist' Shay. Mist' Shay needs his cotton picked jes' as bad as Mist' Deerin'.

Reck'n Mist' Shay'd he'p git David out fo'
hisse'f?"

"I done studied dat. Mist' Shay ain' goin'
tuh fight Mist' Deerin' fo' one nigger. Mist'
Shay borries money f'um Mist' Deerin's bank
an' he cain' mek a enemy o' him."

"Money. Eb'rything's money. If we could
git some money we'd git Jedge Mayna'd tuh
go tuh co't fo' him ——"

"Talk sense, woman," Dee said tiredly.

2

There were cases where niggers in trouble
had gone to white lawyers. Not six months
ago old man Crosby, beyond the sunrise bend,
who had his own eighteen acres, went to law
against a white farmer and all he got was the
lawyer's bill. White lawyers do not care about
niggers who oppose planters, especially influential ones, and there were no nigger lawyers
within a hundred miles of Live Oak. There
was one in Macon and another in Atlanta, nigger lawyers who argued against white lawyers
before white judges and did not get their heads
cracked for impudence; but here in Ochlockonee county white lawyers were unwilling to
oppose white planters in a white man's court.
68

When the mule was unharnessed Dee went to bed. He stared out of the small window panes at the stars low in the sky, sighed and turned restlessly.

" Cain' you sleep, Dee? " Louise asked.

He put his hand out to pat her head as he had done when their mule died and the Lord had not heard their prayers. Her cheeks were wet to his touch.

" Ain' no sense tuh dat," he said kindly.

" De Lawd's done fo'got us, Dee," she wept. " I feel hit in my bones. He's done fo'got us er He neber would a-let dis happen."

" Hush," he chided. " De Lawd neber fo'-gits none o' His chillun. He's jes' busy, woman. He's got other things tuh study wid-out allus studyin' 'bout de Jacksons. He ain' fo'got. No, suh. Doan you neber say dat."

" If dis was Jan'ry de deputies would a-slapped him an' sen' him on home. Now, he'll have tuh stay in jail fo' months fo' co't sets an' den be carried tuh de chain gang."

" You cain' pick cotton in a jail cell. I reck'n Mist' Deerin'll be at de co't house tuh-morrer tuh git 'em tuh sign tuh wuk fo' him."

He sighed and turned again.

" Bes' go tuh sleep now. We got tuh wuk
in de mo'nin'."

4

Ochlockonee's acres were heavy with the
season's yield. Niggers walked the furrows
with bent backs or crawled on knee-pads to
pick the cotton before the skies clouded and
equinoctial rains swept the land. But more
niggers were needed, strong niggers, niggers
who could pick two hundred, two hundred
and fifty pounds and more a day.

The court of general jurisdiction meets
twice a year but white justice sheds its lethargy
when niggers are needed in the cotton fields.

5

On Monday morning, after the five prisoners were fed hominy, molasses and black
coffee, two deputies escorted them to the sheriff. He sat in a large swivel chair before a
roll-top desk.

" What the hell was the matter with you
boys Sat'dee ev'nin'? " he asked genially.
" Cain't you bucks behave yo'se'ves? "

" Cap'n, I didn't——" a nigger began
eagerly.

70

"Yeah, I've heard that befo'. You didn't do nothin' an' nobody else did. There was no fight an' no cuttin' an' no gamblin' an' no trouble. Fact is, you boys wasn't even in the county, was you?"

The prisoners grinned. The deputies grinned.

Nichols spat into a spittoon at his feet, sucked at his teeth thoughtfully, and shook his head.

"Boys, y'all got some serious charges against you an' as the law I cain't do nothin' 'cept hol' you fo' trial. Co't'll set in about fo' months an' the jedges'll let you know if you go free or git fined or go to the chain gang."

"Fo' months!" one exclaimed.

"Yeah." He shrugged his shoulders regretfully. "Shouldn't a-cut up so frisky Sat'dee an' y'all'd a-bin out in the fields this mawin'."

"I wasn't near the place," the Clayton nigger said sullenly.

The sheriff ignored him and continued:

"I don't figger you bucks are a bad lot. I reck'n y'all's jes' a bunch o' fool niggers a li'l giddy in the haid from too much life in you. I don't like to hol' you all this time co'se it'll be months fo' co't sets. An' then maybe you'll

go free anyway or maybe git thuty days fo'
gamblin' an' sixty days fo' fightin' an' maybe
six months fo' resistin' the law. I reck'n
it means 'bout a year fo' y'all git washed
up."

Jim Deering opened the screened door to
the sheriff's office. His puttees were highly
polished and his coat seemed molded to his
shoulders.

"Morning, Sheriff," he said carelessly.
"Sorry I broke in while you were tending to
some business."

Nichols waved a pudgy hand.

"Perfectly all right, Mr. Deerin'. I'll be
through in a minute. Jes' talkin' to this bunch
we picked up Sat'dee ev'nin'."

The planter nodded and strolled to a window overlooking the lawn.

"That's about all, boys," the sheriff con-
cluded. "I'll have to hol' you till co't sets.
Now, while yo're in jail I want you to behave.
Clean yo' cells ev'ry mawnin' ——"

"Plan to keep them here till court meets?"
Deering asked. "That's a pretty bad break
for them, isn't it?"

"Cain't he'p it, Mr. Deerin'. Charges
against 'em o' gamblin', fightin' an' resistin'

72

the law. Giddy niggers, I reck'n, but I got to hol' 'em."

" Nonsense. There's a fight in Live Oak almost every day and crap shooting every night. As for resisting the law I imagine all they did was to try to run away—which is exactly what you or I would have done."

The prisoners stared at him suspiciously.

" Maybe so. Maybe so. They may even git off ——"

" I think it's bad business to feed them for months, bad for the county and bad for them. If they are acquitted it will have cost the county money and if they're found guilty they'll have to work the roads longer to meet the costs that piled up."

" But there's nothin' I kin do about it, Mr. Deerin'," the sheriff said apologetically.

" Of course there is. If you make the charge disturbing the peace they could plead guilty and you would have to bring them before a justice of the peace immediately. He'll probably fine them twenty-five dollars and costs and you'll have it over with."

" We ain' got no money fo' a fine," a prisoner said hesitantly.

" That's so, too."

The prisoners glanced at one another with understanding, worried looks.

" I need help in my fields and I'll pay your fines as advances against your wages," the planter smiled. " I'll help you out of this mess if you'll help me. Thirty dollars a month. In five or six weeks you will have worked off the fine and be free instead of still being in jail waiting for trial."

" Feedin' 'em all these months would be an expense," the sheriff said thoughtfully. He turned to the prisoners. " I don't figger y'all's such a bad lot as I tol' you an' I'm willin' to he'p you an' the county. If you want to accept Mr. Deerin's offer, why I'll change the charges. I don't want to stan' in nobody's way if they want to do you a good turn."

" I wasn't near de place," the Clayton nigger repeated.

" That's fo' the co't to decide," Nichols frowned. " You don't have to plead guilty if you don't want to. Some niggers never appreciate a favor."

" It would be a shame to send these boys to the chain gang," Deering said quietly, " especially now that the Prison Commission will restore the leather again."

74

David had heard old convicts tell of the leather strap whipped across naked buttocks. Its use had been forbidden by law after horrified citizens awoke to its barbaric cruelty. Now it was to be restored. Deering was in a position to know for he was a county commissioner.

The planter glanced at a neat wrist watch.

" What say, boys? " Nichols asked.

" I reck'n I'll sign," one said slowly.

It was obvious to them that the alternative to the chain gang was signing, and one by one they agreed.

There was no difficulty with the justice of the peace. He heard their pleas and imposed fines of twenty-five dollars and costs on each.

When they got into the planter's car his coat flapped back. They saw the shine of a smooth-worn, brown holster.

6

As far as the eyes could see the Deering acres were white with cotton. But no cabin dotted the fields, no bent back picked the whiteness from the crisp bolls. The rich land was deserted but for a slim figure on horseback in the distance, a white man, lean and wiry. A black, felt hat shaded his dark face and a rifle rested across the pommel of his saddle.

Deering slowed down and called:

" Hello, Sam."

" Howdy, Mr. Deerin'," the man returned.

It was high noon when the car turned into a narrow side road. Deep in the fields was a cluster of buildings in a wire inclosure, two large, rambling ones like barrack and mess halls and three shacks, two near the gate entrance and the third beside a gravel road leading to a white mansion rising out of a green sea of lawn a thousand feet away. Beyond the wire fence were barns and shelters and a flat pen filled with fertilizer. A quarter of a mile east other cabins baked in the sun, homely places with spots of green about them and wash hanging on lines stretched between trees.

Two Ford trucks were inside the gate. An odor of manure hung over the stockade.

A gigantic nigger stood with arms akimbo in the doorway of a shack surveying them.

" Charlie! " Deering called to him. " These niggers will work here."

To the boys in the car he said crisply:

" Hop out. Charlie will show you about."

Three horses were hitched under a clump

76

of live oaks in a corner of the stockade. Three niggers with shotguns in their laps lolled lazily on the grass.

" Bettah git'n de mess hall fo' yo' dinnah," Charlie suggested mildly to the newcomers.

VI

NINETEEN niggers were at two long, pine tables. The room smelled of food and perspiration and manure. A solemn-faced wench brought plates of black-eyed peas and chunks of pork, corn bread, tin spoons and tin cups filled with water.

The faces at the tables were resentful, sullen. Sometimes they spoke, in low tones, as though fearful of their own voices. A nigger facing David ate awkwardly with his left hand. The right was bandaged with a dirty rag. A city nigger who had never picked a boll before. He had been on his way to Memphis but he was working for Deering now. The dried leaves, sharp as knives to the inexperienced, had cut his hands until they were raw.

78

When a nigger finished eating he went out to smoke in the shade of the building until it was time to be taken to the field being picked that day.

A leathery-skinned white in puttees and brown, duck trousers and a pistol in a holster on his hip, talked to the newcomers when they went out.

" Charlie'll show you yo're bunks an' fix you up with overalls so's you won't tear your clo'se," he said tersely. " If there's somethin' you want—underwear, shoes, 'baccy, you kin git it from the commissary. Better change now."

Fifteen iron cots with old mattresses and rough, brown blankets, ranged each side of the barracks. The windows were covered with iron netting. In the rear were three stools and near them, six faucets emptying into a sink resembling a trough.

" Dese heah bunks ain' bein' used now," Charlie suggested, pointing them out. " Pick yo'se'f one."

A nigger brought overalls and threw them on a bunk. When the change was made Charlie said:

" Y'all git yo' bags in de trucks. Ah reck'n

79

Mist' Taylah—he's yo' ovahseeah—'ll talk a
bit fo' you go out in de fiel's. He gin'rally do.
Bes' mine 'im, caise he's hahd, hahd'n a string
o' bahbed wiah."

The overseer was waiting for them near the
trucks.

"You new niggers," he began abruptly,
" any o' you never picked cotton befo'? "

" No, suh," one said timidly.

" That's good. Mr. Deerin' specks y'all to
work an' I figgers husky bucks like you kin do
two hunnerd an' fifty poun's a day. Now, you
git the bes' kine o' treatment here. Good food,
an hour an' a half fo' dinner an' plenty o'
water out in the fiel's. Nobody likes a good
nigger better'n Mr. Deerin' or myse'f."

The three niggers with shotguns mounted
their horses. The overseer glanced at them.

" They's some niggers that don't appreciate
good handlin'," he added. " Them guards is
fo' them who try to cheat Mr. Deerin' by gittin' advances an' a lot o' stuff from the commissary an' then runnin' away. Some niggers
is like that, lazyin' on the job an' tryin' to
swindle Mr. Deerin'.

" But I don't figger y'all's that kine, so hop
in. I speck 'bout a hunnerd poun's fo' supper."

80

2

A pile of cotton sacks and a milk can filled
with water was in the center of the truck. The
nigger from the cabin beside the gravel road,
the cook's husband, sat at David's left and
Limpy Rivers at his right, on one of the boards
that served for seats. David was startled to
see Limpy. He had been on the chain gang in
Snake Fork, a surly, grumbling nigger, but
some six weeks before had been counted out
in the morning line. Outside of a casual nod
Limpy did not notice him.

The guards and overseer followed the truck
on horseback.

One of the newcomers glanced at the fields
and said:

"That's sho a lot o' cotton."

"Dey's mo'n dat," the cook's husband volunteered. "Dey's mo' Deerin' niggahs 'bout
three miles east."

David looked at the armed guard following
them.

"Mighty lak a chain gang," he said guardedly.

"You mek yo' time dey an' goes free,"
Limpy growled.

"We cain' go after we wuks out de advance?" David asked, startled.

"Ask Cooky," Limpy returned.

"Mist' Deerin' gimme ten dollahs two years ago. I ain' wukked hit out yet," the cook's husband said.

Two miles from the stockade the trucks entered a clearing in a full-flowering field. Cane brakes in the distance marked the end of the cotton rows. The cans of water were placed beside a weighing machine near which wicker baskets were piled. Each nigger took a bag and a basket and left for the area assigned him. Two guards rode to the cane brakes where a path separated them from the cotton field. The other patrolled the road from the clearing to the highway. The overseer rode the furrows, watching the niggers and returning to the clearing to weigh the full baskets when they were brought in.

Limpy walked with David.

"Some niggers try to run away by gittin' in dem brakes," Limpy said.

"Yeah?" said David.

"De brakes en' up in a big swamp—miles an' miles long."

"Yeah."

" Mos'ly new niggers. Doan know no better. Ain' no sense goin' dey."

" No, no sense in dat."

One hundred pounds before supper meant
fast work and David picked swiftly and
steadily. The sweat under his arms irritated
him. Sweat formed on his upper lip and
trickled to the corners of his mouth, leaving a
salty taste.

3

An hour before sundown the overseer blew
his whistle. The clearing was banked high
with cotton. In the morning the trucks would
take it to the Deering gin.

It was almost dark when the niggers returned to the inclosure lighted by four lanterns
on high poles, and washed the sweat from their
faces at the common trough. After supper
they gathered about the worn steps of the mess
hall and barracks. Few of them talked and
those who did, the burden of their conversa-
tion was women, women they had known and
women they hoped to meet when they got
out.

" If yo're a good nigger an' do yo' weight
Mist' Deerin' gin'rally carries you to town

some Sat'dee ev'nin' or lets you go wid Mist'
Taylor," David learned.

4

Sometimes when they came in from the
fields the overseer would say a pleasant word
or Mr. Deering would smile and tell two or
three they could go to Live Oak on Saturday.
Then the whole atmosphere would change.
They would tell stories, laugh and sing. They
were so grateful for a little kindness.

Mondays were usually pleasant. They were
rested and the fortunate ones who had been to
the county seat were still reliving their experi-
ences with vivid words and exclamations.
Sometimes they talked enviously of the ser-
vants in the big house but the wenches in
starched aprons and white caps were beyond
them. Charlie claimed the prettiest and the
guards claimed the others.

But even talking made them feel a little
closer to the living world.

5

The public school for niggers in Live Oak
had been too far away for David to attend so
he had never learned to read or write. One

evening, on the return from the fields, he asked Cooky if he could write.

" Sho," he said with a touch of pride. " Ah wen' to de fo'th grade."

" I wanted to write tuh my folks," the boy explained.

" Come on ovah after suppah an' Ah'll write hit fo' you. Co'se Ah will."

Thereafter David often visited Cooky. They would sit on the porch, smoke and talk in low tones. Sometimes Mary Lou, his wife, would sit with them and watch her three-year-old son at play.

Once David asked them:

" Why doan you git yo'se'f a passel o' lan' f'um Mist' Deerin' an' maybe you kin mek a li'l money sometimes? "

" Mist' Dee'in' doan wan' croppahs," Cooky explained. " He got 'bout thuty now but dey's mòs'ly niggahs whut's bin dey long befo' he got de lan'. He'd rathah git fam'ly niggahs by de month if he kin, co'se hit's hahd fo'm to run away. But even single men's cheapah by de month co'se in wintah he lets 'em run away an' he doan have to advance 'em ten dollahs a month while de crop's growin'."

David learned his story.

Cooky, whose name was Walter Freedman, had worked in an Alabama mill until he got consumption. A nigger doctor told him to get out in the sun if he wanted to see his boy grow up and the coughing, emaciated nigger went to work for a farmer. At the end of the month he discovered that he was being cheated. That same night Mary Lou and he bundled their few personal belongings in a blanket, took their seven-months-old baby, and crossed the Chattahoochee River into Georgia to avoid trouble with the planter who claimed a debt of eight dollars and thirty-seven cents for goods advanced. An independent nigger farmer was giving them a lift through Ochlockonee county when Deering passed and asked if they were looking for work.

Forty dollars a month for him and his wife were the wages agreed upon and a ten dollar advance sealed the contract. At the end of the first month Freedman's itemized account showed that deducting the value of purchases from the commissary, he had two dollars and eighty-one cents due him, but the clerk's ledger showed a debit balance of over six dollars for him. Deering was in the store looking over the stock and Freedman called his attention to the discrepancies in the two accounts, tendering his own carefully listed figures. The planter silently took the large, red ledger and glanced at the Freedman page.

"That's what the ledger shows," he said frowning.

"Ah didn't buy dat much stuff, suh," Freedman insisted.

"That's what the ledger shows," the planter snapped. "I guess your figures don't include rent and interest on the value advanced you."

"I figgered rent, but I didn't buy dat much stuff. An' dey cain' be eight dollahs int'res'," he protested.

Deering's face flushed. With an angry exclamation he struck him in the mouth, knocking him against a flour barrel.

"You impudent son of a bitch!" he raged. "Do you mean I'm stealing from you!"

Freedman never protested again. Succeeding months found the debt increasing. The planter charged twenty percent interest on the balance as recorded in his books. The latest reckoning showed the nigger almost two hundred dollars in debt.

"Ah'll never pay out," he concluded resignedly. "But, dey all de same, only some is

87

wussen others. But Ah ain' got no mo' cough. Wukkin' in de sun sho fixed dat up fine. An' Ah gits mah clo'se an' food, an' Chrismus time Ah gits ten dollahs Chrismus money an' sometimes Mist' Dee'in' sen's ovah some things fo' li'l Harrison to play wid. Ah wanted to run away again but f'um whut I heahs, places ain' much diff'run' so Ah stays on. Hit could be wuss."

6

There were some who found contentment in the Deering stockade. A man has to work for someone, and once a nigger gets that into his head and does not expect too much he can be happy, so Joe Wallis with his moon face and sunny disposition, was happy. To Joe life was filled with fun and laughter. His presence made things easier and everybody liked him, even the guards and the overseer and Deering.

Joe sang. His round face would wreathe in smiles, his feet would tap time, his head and shoulders would shake and his eyes would roll. Ballads, blues, spirituals. He had a great store of them and when those were not sufficient for his mood, he would make up his own,

88

about little things in the stockade or thoughts
that he had or a wench he had known.

They liked *My Jane* especially and they
always sang it with him:

My Jane, whut a gal! she loves red shoes,
My Jane, whut a gal! she loves silk clo'se.

My Jane, whut a gal! she loves plenty money,
She kin devil a feller till hit ain' even funny.

My Jane, whut a gal! she loves heaps o' men,
Gits whut you got an' dat's yo' en'!

"Ain' dat de truff!" someone always
shrieked.

"Yas, suh, but she's wuth hit!" he inva-
riably replied.

My Jane, whut a gal! drive a feller to de bad,
My Jane, hell-o-mighty! bes' gal I ever had!

But sometimes Joe sang of thoughts none
would dare utter in prosaic talk. Then his
companions would stir restlessly and shake
their heads.

"Dat's right," they would say to one another.

89

Nigger go to white man,
Ask him fo' wuk.
White man say to nigger:
" Git out o' yo' shirt."

Nigger throws off his coat,
Goes to wuk pickin' cotton.
W'en time come to git pay,
White man give 'im nothin'.

Li'l bees suck de blossoms.
Big bees eat de honey.
Nigger raises de cotton an' cawn,
White folks git de money.

When the overseer or the planter were in an ugly mood they did not sing. On such days they lay on their cots talking, often reliving the events that brought them there. One nigger who had come in February had been on his way home from Atlanta to Tallahassee. In Ochlockonee county a deputy saw him on the highway swinging his carefree way. Now he was working for Deering.

" Maybe sometime Mist' Deerin'll git good an' tard o' havin' dis nigger 'roun'," he smiled cheerfully, " an' den maybe I kin go on my way. An' boy, w'en dis nigger gits home he ain' travellin' no mo'! "

90

Limpy told how Deering paid five dollars for him, the balance of a twenty-five dollar fine for vagrancy, to secure his release from the chain gang a month before the sentence was up. Thirty dollars a month he had been promised and in the six weeks he had been on the planter's land he had not yet worked off the five dollar advance. Deering charged him for food, for rent, for shoes, for everything possible.

"Dat's how dey git you," he finished sourly.

"I bin heah five months an' I'se sho' lucky I didn't git mah haid busted," Joe Wallis announced gleefully. "I was standin' fron' o' de drug sto' in Live Oak wid half a pint o' moonshine in mah belly—I was so drunk I couldn't hit de groun' wid mah hat! I said, 'God damn' 'bout somethin' or other w'en a white man an' woman was passin' by an' fo' I knew hit de white man smacked me square in de mouf fo' swearin' befo' a white woman an' de sheriff slapped me in jail—an' heah I is!"

"Yeah. An' here you stay," Limpy assured him dryly.

7

On the day he got Dee's answer to his letter

David was depressed. When Cooky finished reading it the boy shook his head dolefully.

" I reck'n dey keep a nigger here till he jes' has tuh run away," he said.

Freedman sucked thoughtfully at his cold pipe.

" Tain' smaht to run away," he finally said.

" Tain' right tuh keep you locked up lak you was on de chain gang, either."

" Co'se 'tain' right but whut's a wum gonter do w'en a bud got him in his mouf? Hollah ' Hey, Mist' Bud, you ain' got no right to be eatin' me!' Whut do dat git 'im? Git 'im a slap in de mouf, dat's whut hit git 'im. Dat wum cain' argy w'en de bud's eatin' 'im. All he kin do is try to git away. Hollah'n ain' no good. Hell, no! "

" Reck'n a nigger kin git away? " David asked in a low tone.

" Las' yeah Willie Frazer an' Sam Lowie done run away," Freedman said slowly. " Willie'd bin a good niggah fo' a month after he come heah an' den wen' slap out o' his haid. Sudden. Jes' lak dat. Hit was choppin' time an' he'd bin wukkin' all day. Right alongside o' me, too, an' he didn't ack crazy a-tall. But all of a sudden up he straightens an' widout a

wud stahts runnin' fo' de swamps. Mist'
Taylah was dey an' he hollahs fo' him to stop
but Willie jes' kep' right on lak de devil hisse'f was after'm. Mist' Taylah hollahd again
an' den Buck raises his gun an' lets 'im have a
barrel-full.

"We bu'ied 'im in de swamp right dey wid
a weight roun' his laigs to keep'm f'um comin'
up an' hantin' Buck."

"Dey kilt 'im?" David exclaimed.

"Yeah. Buck did. But dat ain' all. Hit
was after dat dat Sam Lowie stahts fussin'
'bout Buck killin' Willie an' de fus' thing he
knows Mist' Dee'in' knocked a couple o' his
teeth out an' Mist' Taylah hit 'im on de haid
wid a pick handle an' den Sam wen' clean out
o' his haid, too. Mus' a-bin de sun dat yeah,
I reck'n. Mus' a-bin, co'se Sam ups one
ev'nin' an' run away. Ain' nobody knows
whut's happened till Mist' Dee'in' brung 'im
back all hog tied an' w'en he gits 'im in de
stockade Charlie gi'm de leather till his ahms
hu't.

"Law', dat was a whippin'. He was laid
up two weeks, he was hu't so bad.

"Sam mus' a-bin clean crazy wid de heat er
stubbo'n as a gov'men' mule co'se you know

93

whut he done? W'en he run away, instead o' keepin' right on goin' dat fool niggah wen' straight to de she'iff's office an' says Buck Robe'ts done kilt Willie an' he seed 'im do hit. Fo' Sam knew whut happened he was slapped in jail an' Mist' Dee'in' noterfied dey had a runaway niggah b'longin' to 'im. An' w'en Mist' Dee'in' got 'im heah, he sho made a mess o' 'im.''

"Whey's Sam now?" David asked, frightened.

"Nobody knows dat. Two days after he could stan' on his two feet he wen' in de fiel's again an' nobody seed him after dat. If dat niggah's gone again he didn't go to de she'iff no mo', dat's sho.''

He puffed at his pipe meditatively.

"Or maybe,'' he added slowly, "he's bu'ied in de swamp, too.''

8

Like a sudden equinoctial storm came the trouble over Limpy Rivers. His sullen bitterness had earned him the reputation of being ugly. Charlie had tried to humble him shortly after he was brought from the convict camp, and failed. The huge nigger had warned him:

94

"Dey ain' no use yo' bein' uppity roun' heah. If yo' behave yo'se'f you'll git along lots bettah."

"Nigger," Limpy had returned harshly, "I'm doin' my work? Den mine yo' own bus'ness an' you'll git along lots better, too!"

There was something about Limpy that discouraged even the guard from pressing him too far.

Limpy did his work. Despite the hip injury that caused the limp, he was one of the best pickers in the stockade. He picked so rapidly that he had leisure to stroll to the clearing frequently for a dipperful of the warm water. Sometimes he spat it out contemptuously.

"That nigger's gonter git in trouble," the overseer remarked once.

One morning Limpy refused to get up saying he was sick. Taylor and Deering came and though he did not look sick, said nothing. Then, on a day when the sun seemed bent on shriveling everything in the fields and clothes stuck to sweating bodies, Limpy lay down beside a rivulet that ran thinly through a field and drank a bellyful of the cool water. A few

95

days later, when the crews were awakened in the morning, his head swam and he lay back.

"I got de mis'ries," he said when Charlie came to see why he was not up.

"Yeah? You played sick befo'. Say, you bin tryin' awful hahd to git in trouble roun' heah f'um de fus' day you come an' now you stahtin' in to play sick reg'lah, eh? Bettah git up fo' Mist' Taylah obliges you wid somethin' to git de mis'ries ovah."

"I got de mis'ries, nigger!" Limpy said angrily. "Hush yo' big mouf an' git me a doctor."

"You got too damn much mouf fo' a sick niggah! Git up or I'll repo't you to Mist' Taylah."

Limpy looked at him with hatred and turned his head. Charlie left and returned with the overseer. Breakfast was almost over when Limpy appeared with a rapidly swelling lip. He swallowed a mouthful of coffee but did not touch the food. Taylor and the guard watched him from the doorway, their faces grim.

When the crews straggled out of the mess hall and Taylor shouted, "Pile in!" Limpy took his place in the truck, holding his head

96

in his hands. Once he shivered as with a chill.

When the trucks returned for the noon meal Taylor spoke to Deering and the two watched him walk to the mess hall and slump against the screen door. The planter went to him quickly.

"What's the matter with you?" he asked coldly.

"I got de mis'ries bad, awful bad, Mist' Deerin'," Limpy said weakly.

"Mr. Taylor tells me you were lazying in the fields all morning." Deering clipped the words.

"I got de mis'ries, Mist' Deerin'. I'm willin' to work but I got a fever dat's bun'in' me all up an' makin' me shiver half de time. I cain' work. I wisht you'd git me a doctor."

"I'm not paying you to get fever!" Deering exploded. "You've been too damned uppity from the day you got here. You're always hunting trouble and if you hunt a little more, you'll find it! Now, if you don't want to go in there and eat, that's your lookout, but I don't want to hear of any more trouble over you. You get out in the fields and do your share!"

"I got de mis'ries bad, Mist' Deerin',"

97

Limpy repeated. He held on to the wall for
support. " I doan wan' no trouble. I got de
mis'ries. Cain' you see I got 'em?"

Deering ignored him.

" Let me know if he does his work," he said
to Taylor.

" Sho," said Limpy bitterly, " if I was yo'
slave an' you paid a t'ousan' dollars fo' me
you'd tek care o' me w'en I git de mis'ries but
you kin git plenty mo' niggers cheap if I
die ——"

Deering turned on him white with fury.
His fist smashed against the nigger's face.
Limpy sank to the ground, blood running
from his nose and mouth. He wiped his chin
with a hand and looked at it dazedly.

" I got de mis'ries, Mist' Deerin'. I ain'
lazyin' on you, suh."

" Get up and go to work!" Deering ordered
tensely. " Get up, or I'll give you something
to get sick over!"

Limpy's eyes flared.

" Sho," he growled, " why doan you kill me
now instead o' sendin' me out in de fiel's to
die!"

The planter's face turned apoplectic. For
a moment he tried to restrain himself. Then,

98

with a swift movement his hand darted to his hip and drew his pistol.

With a hoarse scream Limpy tried to scramble to his feet, his hands half raised in supplication.

" Mist' Deerin'——" he cried.

Deering fired twice. Limpy slumped to the ground, his head on his chest. His hands lay loose in his lap as though he had fallen asleep.

" You asked for it, you black bastard!"

The planter swung the door open.

" I want no impudence around here!" he shouted to the terrified niggers at the tables. " Remember that! And I'm not paying you to play sick. I'm paying you to work!"

He turned to the gigantic nigger beside him.

" Weight the son of a bitch and bury him in the swamp!"

VII

GUARDS and overseer rode grimly, and Deering niggers moved from stalk to stalk, silent and apprehensive.

A fear he had not felt even on the chain gang was in David's heart. There, convicts were punished. One, who had tried to escape, died while being punished but no one had been killed for impudence. In Snake Fork there were niggers who, rightly or wrongly, were convicted of crimes but here there were only niggers who had accepted a few dollars from Deering. Dee's father had brought eighteen hundred dollars in the open market and no man throws eighteen hundred dollars into a swamp in a fit of anger, but Limpy had cost Deering only five dollars. Five dollars. That was all. And there were lots of five dollar niggers, five dollar niggers and twenty-five dollar niggers to be taken from jails and chain gangs or hired for an advance. None cost a thousand dollars or eighteen hundred dollars. Cheap niggers—and the south was full of them, ploughing the soil, chopping cotton, picking cotton, ginning cotton. And if Limpy were never seen again, why, he was just a nigger who owed Deering money and ran away, a runaway nigger afraid to show his face; and if someone told the sheriff—well, look at what happened to Sam Lowie.

2

" Keep yo' mouf shut an' ack lak nothin's happened," Cooky advised David when they returned from the fields.

No one spoke of Limpy. It was hard to believe that this noon he had opened his mouth and this evening he was in a dismal swamp, dead, with weights around his body. Their feet were heavy on the mess hall floor. The clatter of cups and plates sounded harsh. Some tried to speak, casual talk of food and dung flies buzzing about them, but their voices were strained, unnatural. On their cots in the barracks they tossed restlessly. Mattresses rustled and beds creaked and shadows of the window netting threw tiny squares on them and the walls and the floor.

A nigger on a cot near David whispered:

"I kin still see 'im, squattin' dey, an' him jes' kilt."

Joe Wallis uttered a high, nervous laugh.

"Boy," he announced earnestly, "dis ain' no place fo' li'l Joe Wallis. W'en dey starts killin' us, dat's w'en li'l Joe starts follerin' de road f'um here to anywhey!"

"Hit'll be a long time fo' I fo'git de way dat Limpy man looked," a voice said fearfully.

"Fo'git 'im!" Joe exclaimed loudly. "Lawd, I'd know him if I saw his ashes in a whirlwin'!"

A nigger turned upon him irritably.

"Hush yo' big mouf," he advised sharply. "Dis ain' no time fo' talkin'."

In the morning Joe Wallis was gone.

How he slipped out they could not guess. His absence was immediately reported and though neither Deering nor Taylor commented upon it, the tension over the stockade grew. At breakfast, in the trucks and in the fields, they were glum, nervous, fearful. Each

102

order, each command was given sharply, harshly.

High Yaller, who had been in the stockade two months, a quiet nigger who minded his own business, threw his sack down and started for the clearing.

"Hey, you! What the hell's the matter with you!" Taylor shouted.

The nigger stopped. He turned and picked up his bag.

"I reck'n you cain' even git a drink now no mo'," he said sullenly.

When the trucks returned for the noon meal Taylor sent a mule boy to the commissary for Deering. The planter came, his face drawn and his jaws clenched. Through the mess hall door they saw Taylor whisper to Deering.

"Mo' trouble," a nigger said in an undertone.

"Heah dey come," another voice said.

Deering, with Taylor and the guards behind him, kicked the door open. The planter was tense, almost quivering with fury. The strain on him since the killing seemed at the breaking point. The niggers stopped eating and stared dumbly at him.

"All of you!" he called harshly. "Pile out!"

One rose hastily. The others followed, crowding each other.

"High Yaller!" Deering called.

The nigger's shoulders were hunched like an animal about to spring when he stepped from the group.

"I told you yesterday I want no impudent niggers on my farm!" the planter said savagely to the huddled group. They had never seen him so furious, not even when he shot Limpy. "Now you're going to see what happens to those who think they can get impudent!"

High Yaller straightened up. The watching niggers could not see his face but they saw his fists clench and quickly open again lest it be misunderstood.

"Charlie! And you, Pete! Strip this son of a bitch and give him twenty lashes!"

"Mistuh," High Yaller said evenly, "am I gonter git whipped fo' wantin' a drink o' water?"

Deering ignored him. A guard slipped handcuffs on him. Another appeared with a long, leather strap of knotted thongs. With a

104

quick movement the guards threw him face down. One sat on his shoulders and the other on his feet. Charlie slipped the nigger's overalls down until the buttocks were exposed, took the strap and stepped back. It swished through the air and cracked like a pistol shot on the brown flesh.

High Yaller screamed and squirmed, rubbing his face in the soil. The guards dug their feet into the earth to keep from being thrown off.

Red welts showed on the skin.

The strap swished through the air again.

High Yaller ceased screaming before the twentieth stroke. He moaned and his body jerked spasmodically. His face was scratched and bleeding. He tried to spit the red clay from his mouth but it stuck to his lips and chin.

The exposed flesh was a mass of welts and criss-crossed lines of blood.

A guard unlocked the handcuffs. The nigger rose unsteadily, the overalls falling about his feet. He took a step forward and fell.

They carried him to the barracks and laid him face down on his cot.

Flies settled on the raw buttocks.

3

Madness descended upon the stockade. The slightest infraction of an order was met with a curse or a beating. Once David did not move fast enough and a guard hurled a pick handle at him. Such talk as there was by bolder spirits was in guarded undertones and the undercurrent of fear and hate only added to the tension.

The fields were still heavy with cotton. Two niggers were gone and one too badly hurt to work. Two days after High Yaller's whipping four niggers who had been threatened rushed for the swamps in a concerted move. Taylor shouted and cursed but did not raise his gun. He did not even try to capture them.

Each runaway reduced the daily weight. Much of the first picking had not been touched. The fields already worked were almost ready for a second picking, and niggers were running away.

Deering went to Live Oak and returned with a new batch of six.

4

David concluded that a convict suit could

not be worse than Deering overalls but he hesitated to run away. He would never dare set foot in Ochlockonee county again if he did.

One quiet evening on Cooky's porch the boy asked abruptly:

"Figger Mist' Pearson'd pay de res' o' my fine?"

"How you git to 'im?"

"I figgered maybe I'd ask Mist' Deerin' tuh let Mist' Pearson pay hit."

"Yeah? Mist' Deerin' ain' lettin' nobody go w'en he's so late wid his pickin'."

The boy sighed.

"Maybe I could run away," he said slowly.

"Yeah. Maybe."

"Pete wen' after me wid a pick handle day fo' yestiddy."

"Yeah. I saw hit."

"Said he'd beat my God damn haid in."

Freedman nodded sympathetically.

"Ain' no sense stayin' here tuh git my haid beat in."

"No. You right dey. An' dey ain' no sense gittin' wuss if you git caught."

"Whut's a nigger tuh do?" David asked helplessly.

Freedman spat carefully.

"Run away," he said.

"But you done said ——"

"Yeah. Dat's whut I done said. An' I still say dey ain' no sense gittin' wuss if you git caught. Howsomevah, dey ain' no sense stayin' heah, neithah. You's young an' b'long to Mist' Pearson. Maybe he'll he'p you. An' maybe he won't. Hit's a gambelin' chance anyway."

"If I kin git home maybe I kin see Mist' Pearson. I'm willin' tuh wuk, but I doan see no sense in wukkin' fo' a cracked haid."

Freedman stared gloomily at Charlie sitting alone at his shack door.

"If I was younger ——" he began. He did not finish the sentence.

"You'd go wid me?" David asked eagerly. "Why doan you? Whut you got tuh stay fo'?"

"Whey'll I go?"

He shook his head.

"No, dey ain' nothin' I kin do."

He puffed nervously at his pipe.

"But maybe you kin mek hit." He glanced at the guard as though fearful of being overheard. "Yeah. Maybe you kin mek hit."

108

Mary Lou joined them.

"Whut yo' conspirin' about?" she demanded. "Y'all look serious enough to be figgerin' on runnin' away."

"Dat's jes' whut we was figgerin'," Freedman said guardedly.

"Man!" she exclaimed. "You gone clean out o' yo' haid? Whut you mean messin' roun' wid dat idee? Whut you gonter do wif me an' li'l Harrison? Whey we go? Whey we eat an' sleep? How we git outer dis heah county? You crazy?"

Her husband nodded in agreement.

"Runnin' away ain' fo' a man wid a wife an' chile," she continued excitedly. "You cain' even git outer dis county wifout bein' ketched an' all you'll git'll be a whippin'. Hit's alright fo' a boy to run away. He kin sleep in de woods or de swamps, but man, you cain' tek a chile inter no swamps."

"Whut we gonter do?" he asked. "Stay heah fo' de res' o' our life?"

"You gotter stay some place. Nobody's mekkin' you no trouble. Whut you wan' to go lookin' fo' hit fo'? You got a house an' wuk

an' food an' clo'se. Whut you wan'? A
thousan' dollars? "

Freedman did not answer. She turned to
David.

" W'en you fixin' to go? "

" Fus' chance I git. Ain' no sense stayin'
heah waitin' tuh git beat up."

" No. I reck'n dey ain'. Dat's right."

" I'd go dis minute if I had a chance."

" Law', dey's plenty chances. Jes' tell
Charlie you got a date wif one o' de gals up
at de big house. He let you go, an' you jes'
keeps right on goin'."

" Yeah? An' Charlie'll say ' Whey's dat
gal? W'en you git a chance tuh date her up? '
an' den I git slapped all aroun'."

" Yeah. Dat's right." She nodded sympathetically. " I tell you whut. You bin comin'
here an' mekkin' my ackquentance. You tell
him you got a date wif me."

Freedman looked up, startled.

" We gotter he'p dis boy," she explained.
" If niggers doan he'p each other, whey dey
git he'p? "

" Yeah. I reck'n dat's right," he said
thoughtfully.

" Sho. Tell Charlie you got a date wif me.

Den w'en Walter goes to bed I walks out in de woods so Charlie kin see me. You ask him if you kin go. We nacherly cain' come back together. I come back alone, an' hit ain' my fault if you doan come back."

"Den Charlie'll git fresh wif you," her husband objected.

"He'll git his haid busted right quick if he do," she laughed.

Freedman knocked the ashes from his cold pipe into the palm of a hand.

"Well, I reck'n if yo' fixin' to go, you'd bes' go," he said quietly. "I sho hope you mek hit."

"Doan shake han's," she cautioned quickly. David rose.

"You git back to de barracks," she advised. "W'en you see me goin' out, you foller. I'll be waitin' near de fo' live oaks yonder on de road. But mine, ask Charlie."

David's heart pounded with fear when he approached the guard. The boy tried to walk with an air of casualness.

"Reck'n I kin go yonder later?" he asked, pointing with a thumb to the road.

"Wha' fo'?"

"Jes'—jes' ——" David forced a nervous grin.

"I bin speckin' you, boy," Charlie chuckled. "You bin hangin' roun' dat cabin too much. Cooky'll bus' yo' haid wide open if you ain' keerful."

David swallowed hard.

"He'll be asleep," he managed to say.

"Ain' a bad wench a-tall," the guard continued expansively. "Ain' bad a-tall." David could smell moonshine on his breath. "Well, if you gits yo'se'f a woman hit ain' fo' me to stop you!"

"Den I kin go?" the boy asked eagerly.

"Sho! An' I'll gi' you a drink fo' you go, too! Come on in heah."

David followed him into the cabin. The guard fumbled in a corner and produced a bottle. Both took long swallows.

"Cain' nobody say Charlie ain' human," the guard said.

The boy returned to the barracks. Stars glowed in the sky and the lanterns covered the stockade with a mellow light. He rolled cigarette after cigarette nervously.

Mary Lou's dark figure came out of her cabin and passed the guard's shack.

112

David heard his steps on the hard clay. He wanted to look back when he passed the gate but restrained himself. He strolled leisurely up the road to the clump of live oaks tall against a distant background of wood.

Mary Lou stepped out of the shadows.

" Here you is, boy! " she called cheerfully.

She took his arm. " Here's de path," she explained, pointing to a faint width at their feet. "Hit tu'ns roun' an' gits off three ways."

She stood close to him. Her hips touched his.

" Boy! " she exclaimed with a high giggle. "Whut you shakin' lak dat fo'? You ain' scairt, is you? "

" No," he said.

" I reck'n I'd bes' show you so's you cain' git los'," she announced.

She took his hand. They walked into a tangle of uncultivated land. She threw her arms about him. Her breasts were warm and pliant and her breath hot on his face.

" I reck'n we'll start you off right," she laughed. " If you's gonter have a date wif me you might jes' as well have hit! "

VIII

NINETEEN miles to the county seat but only sixteen to home, and the road to Live Oak clear between fields of dun colored cotton. Travelers were infrequent even in daytime and at night the highway was a wide ribbon of deserted clay. David left mile upon mile behind him. There was exhilaration in the new freedom. Once, in the early hours of the morning, the approaching rumble of a car warned him to stretch out in a ditch at the side of the road.

He was still wide awake when a tiny square of light in a cabin leaning against a deep, purple sky told him that morning was not far away. He scanned the fields anxiously for a safe spot to spend the day and at the first glimmer of a gray dawn struck rapidly

114

through soft furrows towards a horizon of trees beyond a picked field.

The sun was high when he awoke. The grass on which he lay was tall and pleasantly soft. The trees were alive with the chatter of birds. Patches of sunlight. Fields visible through trees. And no cotton to be picked.

The need of water was troublesome by night. The temptation to seek it at the first silhouette of a cabin was strong but the fear that it might be a Cracker or some nigger cropper who would turn him in to curry favor with Deering dissuaded him. Cabins became more frequent and when he saw Lem Haskin's house, with its square barn and the shelters beside it, he knew he was only three miles from home.

Near the broom weeds lining the mule path David listened intently for some sound of guard or deputy waiting in the shadows but only crickets chirping of hot weather on the morrow disturbed the stillness. He glided to the shadows of the house and tapped softly on the window pane of the room where his father and mother slept.

"Who dat?" he heard Louise's startled call.

Dee's quick voice almost smothered the question.

"Dat's David! Doan talk so loud, woman!"

"Hit's me," the boy said softly. "Anybody roun'?"

"Ain' nobody here, Son. Come roun' tuh de do'."

His father let him in quickly. His mother, in a frayed nightgown over her underwear, clasped him to her, crying happily.

"Stop fussin' wid him," Dee grumbled. "He's tard. Cain' you see he's tard? Better stop yo' weepin' an' git him somethin' tuh eat."

She released the boy and started fumbling with the lamp.

"Whut's de matter wid you, woman!" Dee exclaimed irritably. "You out o' yo' haid? Doan you mek no light!"

"I want some water fus'," David said.

"Sho! Sho!" His father pattered to the water bucket. "Lawd, I mus' be gittin' foolisher'n yo' mammy fo' not thinkin' about hit. Co'se you want water. P'obly ain' had nothin' tuh drink sense you run away."

David gulped the water and Dee refilled the cup, moving with eager restlessness in his excitement, a ghostly pair of underwear in the darkness. Trembling questions tumbled from his mother, an eager torrent that did not wait for an answer.

"Hush!" Dee interrupted. "Let de boy eat. Lawd, why did You gib me such a fool woman! Cain' you see he ain' had nothin' tuh eat fo' two days?"

Louise became quiet, leaning on the table, watching her son.

"We knowed you done run away," Dee said. "De sheriff an' a deputy was here at sunup an' said you done run away yestiddy ev'nin'. I tol' 'em I didn't know nothin' 'bout dat but dey suched de place."

"Maybe dey'll come back. You cain' figger 'em out," his mother cautioned.

"I didn't see nobody," David said assuringly. "I was mighty careful fo' I come roun' tuh de window."

"Maybe so. Maybe so," his father said quietly. "But you eat an' tek a mess o' food wid you an' git out in de woods w'ile I study whut tuh do. Cain' be too keerful. Dat man Deerin's gontuh try tuh git you back tuh show de county niggers hit ain' smart tuh run away."

117

Louise began to cry.

"Whut's ailin' you!" Dee turned upon her. "Good Lawd, I never did see such a fool woman!"

"Hit's never seein' Son no mo'," she wept. "He cain' stay here now. Dey'll 'res' 'im an' sen' 'im tuh de chain gang or back again tuh Mist' Deerin's place. Lawd, whut'd You go an' do tuh dis here fam'ly?"

"Hit's a lot better not tuh see 'im no mo' den tuh see his fun'ral," Dee said grimly. "Dat Deerin' place's bad. Bad."

"Yeah," said David. "Dat man'd jes' as soon kill a nigger as spit. He killed one while I was dey."

"Gawd a-mighty!" his mother exclaimed.

"Hush yo' mouf!" Dee cautioned angrily.

"Lawd," she wept, "hit might a-bin him."

"Yeah, hit might a-bin. Dey wen' after me wid a pick handle, once."

"Lawd, Lawd," she breathed, shaking her head.

David explained briefly why he fled. "Dat place ain' fit fo' nobody," he concluded rebelliously. "De chain gang's better'n dat."

"Yeah," said Dee slowly.

"Reck'n Mist' Pearson'd buy me back an'

118

lemme wuk hit out wid you?" David asked anxiously.

"I dunno. I reck'n not. Dey was Bill Huston. He was a Pearson nigger but two years ago w'en Mist' Deerin' couldn't git nobody tuh wuk fo' him he tuk him wid a gun an' Bill, he run away tuh Mist' Pearson but nothin' come of hit. Mist' Deerin's pow'ful strong here'bouts. I reck'n Mist' Pearson ain' gittin' intuh no fight wid him."

"Whut's de boy gontuh do?" Louise asked tearfully.

"I dunno. I got tuh study hit, got tuh do some tall studyin'. But de fus' thing is fo' him tuh git some pone an' pork an' a pot-full o' water an' git out in de woods an' stay dey tuhmorrer till hit's dark."

Louise bundled the food and filled a small iron cooking pot with water.

"Bes' git movin'," Dee suggested. "An' come back here w'en hit's dark."

2

News of a runaway spreads quickly in a land so isolated that everything is a matter of gossip.

The Pearson overseer wandered out to Dee

that morning, spat a mouthful of tobacco juice
on a furrow, and said:

"I hear David done run away f'um the
Deerin' place."

"Yes, suh," Dee said. "De sheriff was
roun' lookin' fo' him."

"Pretty hard man, Mr. Deerin'."

"Yes, suh. Dat's whut I hears."

"Bad place." He squinted at a distant
field. "I hope he gits away," he added
slowly.

"Thank-ee, suh. Thank-ee," Dee said.

During the day Louise cried repeatedly.
Once he nodded sympathetically.

"Sho," he said, "you go right on weepin'.
Hit's nachral fo' a woman."

"Dey might a-killed him."

"Yeah. But dey didn't, an' now he's safe
an' maybe by tuh-morrer he'll be outuh dis
county."

"An' I'll neber see him no mo'."

"Cain' tell," he said hopefully.

3

At sundown Dee fed the mule and left him
harnessed outside the barn. When the supper
dishes were washed and Zebulon put to bed,

120

the three sat on the porch. Louise wanted to extinguish the lamp in the kitchen but Dee shook his head.

"Jes' set aroun' lak allus," he advised. "Dey's nobody roun' but somebody might come roun'."

Dee smoked in silence. Louise rocked nervously in her chair, rattling a loose board in the porch.

"Cain' you set still?" he growled. "Allus movin' an' rockin'! Nuf noise tuh mek a man like tuh slap you!"

"I ain' neber gontuh see him no mo'," she wept.

"Oh, hush! He'll be here. Good Lawd, woman, I wisht de Lawd could a-gib you mo' sense!"

"Whut we gontuh do?" she asked.

"I dunno. I bin studyin' hit all day. Mist' Pearson ain' gontuh he'p but maybe Mist' Ramsey will. He allus he'ps Ramsey niggers an' de Jacksons was Ramsey niggers. My father played wid Mist' Ramsey's father fo' we was freed."

The mule moved restlessly, champing at the bit.

"Whut you gontuh do wid dat mule?"

121

"Maybe I'll ride him tuh Live Oak dis eb'nin'," he returned absently.

"Wid David?"

"You got 'bout as much sense as Zebulon," he said. "I reck'n hit's time fo' you tuh go tuh bed, Henrietta."

The girl got up without a word. Dee followed her in. He removed the chimney from the lamp, pinched the wick between thumb and forefinger, and returned to the porch.

"I reck'n you'd bes' git outuh dat chair an' stop rockin'," he suggested.

For half an hour they sat in silence, Dee puffing at his pipe and sheltering the glow with a cupped hand.

Louise whispered:

"Maybe he didn't wait in de woods."

"He waited. Hush."

"I'm scairt ——"

"Woman," Dee said tensely, "if you doan hush dat mouf o' yourn I'll slap yo' teeth out right now!"

She became silent. The minutes dragged. Suddenly she touched Dee's arm and pointed to the barn.

"Dey he is," she whispered excitedly.

"Son," he said when David joined them,

" dat was fine. If you walk lak dat in de night dey ain' nobody gontuh ketch you. Yes, suh, dat was fine."

" You better he'p him an' not talk so much," Louise interrupted.

" Sho," he said good-naturedly. " I jes' waited fo' him tuh come fo' I lef'. Now, Son, you git yo'se'f some mo' water an' a mess o' food an' git ober tuh dat bale shelter caise maybe I'll be wantin' you dis eb'nin'. I'm gontuh town an' w'en I git back I want tuh know jes' whey you is."

He turned to his wife. "An' you stay right here on de po'ch an' let dat boy sleep. If anybody comes you shout louder'n at prayer meetin' who dey is. Dat'll wake him up an' he kin slip out o' de shelter. I doan figger nobody'll come but I want tuh be keerful."

" Sho I'll wait," Louise said contentedly. " I couldn't go tuh sleep nohow now."

4

The driveway to the spacious Ramsey mansion, little changed from the days when Dee's father played there, was heavy with the odor of jasmine and rose. Two dogs barked at the wagon's approach. Old Brigadier Joe, white

123

haired and neat in his dark suit, switched on the lights of the kitchen porch and peered out.

"Git away f'um heah!" he shouted to the dogs. "Cain' y'all see hit's jes' a ol' niggah? Go on now, git back to yo' kennels! Whut you wan', Dee?" he added, recognizing him. "Doan you know no better'n to come heah at dis time o' de eb'nin'? Whut's de matter wif you?"

"I had tuh come," Dee said apologetically. "I got tuh see Mist' Ramsey."

"Whut's de mattah? You got mo' trouble? Law', you got mo' trouble'n any seben niggahs!"

"I got tuh see Mist' Ramsey," Dee repeated. "Please tell 'im I'm here."

"Sho! Sho! Jes' come right on in an' set down. Mus' be trouble, I reck'n. You look lak de debbil had you by de tail wid a downhill pull on you."

The servant returned quickly.

"You come wif me," he said. "I fixed hit fo' you an' he'll see you right now in de library."

A broad stairway shiny from decades of hard polishing led to the room where the

124

planter sat in an easy chair with a book in his lap.

"Come in, Dee," he smiled kindly. "It must be pretty serious to bring you here at this hour. Someone in trouble again?"

"Yes, suh. Hit's mighty serious, suh. Hit's David."

"H'm." He nodded to the waiting servant. "That will be all, Brigadier. I'll ring when I want you."

Ramsey lighted a cigar, frowning.

"I heard he was working for Deering," he said.

"Yes, suh. But he done run away."

"Why did he do that? He knew he would get into trouble, didn't he?"

"He jes' had tuh run away, suh. A guard wen' at'm wid a pick handle an' dey's beaten 'em all up. 'Bout fo' or five run away already. Dey couldn't stan' hit no mo'."

"Oh. That bad, eh?"

"An' David, he was scairt dey would kill him, too. Mist' Deerin' kilt one nigger an' had him buried in a swamp."

Ramsey chewed vigorously on his cigar.

"Dat's why he run away, suh."

"I think David did wisely," the white man

said quietly. " But what do you want me to do, Dee? Deering isn't the only planter mistreating nigras. I cannot help every darky who finds a hard master."

" Please, suh. David's a good boy. I know dat, eben if he was on de chain gang. He's willin' tuh wuk. He neber did gib nobody no trouble a-tall till dey picked 'im up las' year, an' now mos' eb'rything seems tuh tu'n out all wrong. He's wukked off mos' o' de fine Mist' Deerin' paid fo' him. I doan wan' de boy tuh run away up no'th whey we cain' neber see him no mo'. Maybe he cain' eben git up no'th. Maybe somebody else'll pick 'im up an' sen' him tuh another farm or maybe de chain gang again. Eb'rybody wants cotton pickers. Please, suh, cain' you buy David f'um Mist' Deerin' an' let'm wuk fo' you? You done he'ped a lot o' us niggers, I know. De Jacksons, suh, was allus Ramsey niggers an' ——"

" Yes, I know. There is no need of going into that."

The frown grew deeper between his eyes.

" Why do all you darkies come to me! " he exclaimed. " I can't take care of all the nigras in the south! "

126

Dee's face grew haggard. He slipped from the chair to his knees with hands raised in mute appeal. Before he could utter a word Ramsey called irritably:

"Here! Here! Get up! How the devil do you expect me to think with you down there on your knees!"

"But, suh," Dee pleaded, "cain' you please buy 'im back an' let him wuk hit off fo' you on yo' farm, suh?"

"No! And for heaven's sake, get up! I can't do that, Dee. I have more nigras than I can really take care of."

"Mist' Ramsey," Dee cried despairingly. He rose to his feet, twisting his hat nervously. "Den he's got tuh git out o' dis county, suh! Hit won't do no good tuh tek him tuh Mist' Pearson ——"

"Yes, I know."

"No, suh. If he could git out o' de county, maybe tuh a mill town —— Oh, please, suh, you t in good tuh us niggers an' dey ain' nobody we kin go tuh, suh. Dey'll kill David if dey eber git 'im back on dat farm."

Ramsey stared at the distracted nigger and chewed on his cigar.

"I cain' do nothin', suh. I got tuh wuk in

127

de fiel's till sundown an' if I go dey'll ketch him, sho, an' if David walks out o' de county ——"

"Have you any money?" the planter asked abruptly.

"Yes, suh," Dee said eagerly. "I got fo' dollars an' I'll gib dat tuh him. We ain' needin' no money, suh. All I'm axin' is a li'l he'p tuh git him outuh dis county—maybe tuh Alabama ——"

"It's just as bad there," Ramsey interrupted. "You better hold on to your four dollars. You might need it yourself. I'll give him a few dollars to keep him until he finds a job. Now, I'll help you, but I don't want you to tell all the nigras in the county that I did or I'll have a swarm on my hands and a lot of trouble from the Crackers."

Dee fell to his knees again and seizing Ramsey's hand began to kiss it, sobbing, "Thank-ee, suh, thank-ee."

"Here!" the white man exclaimed, pulling his hand away. "Don't be a damned fool!"

"No, suh! No, suh! I'm sorry, suh!" He rose to his feet and wiped his eyes.

"Have him here at breakfast time."

"In de mo'nin'?"

128

" Yes. I'll take him out of the county my-self. Just have him here."

5

It was a tearful parting for Louise.

" Ain' no sense takin' on lak dat," Dee said. " Hit might be a lot wussen hit is. He might a-bin killed or hu't pretty bad. Lawd, my grandfather was sold a week after I was bo'n an' he neber did set eyes on his chillun again. An' he didn't go tuh weepin'."

He walked with David to the Ramsey fields. It was safer, for though it was not as fast, niggers a-foot can hide easier than a mule and a creaking wagon, if necessary.

At the driveway they paused in the dark shadows of a hedge.

" I reck'n we'd bes' res' here till hit's time," Dee said. " You bes' git yo'se'f some sleep. I'll set up an' call you w'en hit's time."

An hour before sunrise he touched the boy gently.

" I reck'n I'll be leabin' you, Son," he said. " I gottuh be gittin' back tuh wuk."

He caressed the boy's face, something he had not done since David was a child.

" Son, I'm sho sorry tuh see you go. We'll

129

be kind o' worryin' 'bout you so doan you fo'git
us. An' w'en you git out an' settles down some
place, hit'd be right nice if you got some
preacher tuh write a letter fo' you an' tell us
whey you is."

He paused uncertainly and raised his head
to the sky studded with stars. Tears long re-
pressed trickled down his cheeks.

"Son, I'm gibin' you intuh de han's o' de
Lawd ——"

IX

LIVE OAK drowsed in its week-day som-
nolence. A few whites on the sidewalks
looked at the stern Ramsey in the back of his
car and David and the driver in front and
raised forefingers in salutation to the planter.
They reached the open highway unhurriedly
but seven miles out of the county seat a dusty
Ford overtook them and Dan Nichols honked
its horn loudly, motioning the Ramsey car to
the side of the road.

" Pull up," the planter ordered sharply.

" Mornin', sir," the sheriff said without getting out of his car. He nodded towards David.
" That nigger, sir—I have a warrant for his
arrest."

" So I understand, but I'm taking him to
Atlanta with me to see the governor."

131

"What fo'?" Nichols asked in surprise.

"To prefer charges against Deering for murder!" he snapped. "It's about time these disreputable whites were held responsible for their acts!"

David was terrified. A wave of resentment swept over him that this man to whom he looked for help should endanger him. He wanted to deny any such intention but Ramsey's determined air and tightly clipped words frightened him as much as the sheriff's frown.

Nichols leaned easily against his steering wheel.

"Ain't you a li'l hasty, sir?" he asked suggestively. "The Governor—an' I respect him highly, sir—cannot supersede me unless I have failed to do my duty. If this nigger has any charges I'll hear them from him or anyone else."

"I prefer to deal directly with the Governor," Ramsey said coldly.

"That is something, of course, for you to decide. But I took an oath of office an' I inten' to keep it. I cannot permit a man charged with a crime in this county to leave unless he is bailed. I have no charges against Mr.

132

Deerin' before me, but I have got a warrant for this boy. I would appreciate it, sir, if you let me have my prisoner."

"I'll go this nigra's bond," Ramsey said shortly.

"Then we'll return to the county court house."

"I'll follow you."

Nichols nodded and with a "Thank you," turned his car.

"Mist' Ramsey ——" the terrified boy began.

"That's alright, David. Don't worry. You will be released on bail."

"Yes, suh," said David miserably.

Were it not for his father's faith in the man returning him to the law and whose kindness to blacks was common gossip the boy would have risked jumping from the car in a desperate effort to escape the law he had learned to dread. He had heard tales of this law, on the chain gang and on the Deering farm, a just law when black and black were involved but a white man's law when it was black against white. "Trials doan mean nothin'," Limpy Rivers had once said. "You's guilty fo' you come fo' de judge."

133

In the sheriff's office Ramsey motioned the boy to a chair and asked:

" What is the bail, Sheriff? "

" The justice of the peace will have to set it, sir, but I sent Jess Pitkin out to locate'm. In the meantime I'll lock this nigger up pending arrangement for bail."

Ramsey's face flushed.

" I am responsible for him." There was a hard ring to his voice. " I do not think it is necessary to lock him up."

Nichols smiled quickly.

" Very well, sir, if you are responsible. Jess ought to be back right quick. I've telephoned Mr. Deerin' an' Mr. Pearson an' they'll be along. I figgered you'd want to talk to 'em since he's originally a Pearson nigger."

Ramsey shrugged his shoulders indifferently.

" I do not see what interest they could possibly have in him. Mr. Pearson permitted him to be taken away by Mr. Deering and the boy ran away from Deering."

Nichols spat into the spittoon at his feet.

" Perhaps this whole difficulty can be straightened out," he suggested amiably.

134

"To avoid a murder charge against your political backer?" Ramsey asked sharply.

The sheriff shook his head and smiled.

"I'm sure you don't want trouble in your own community, Mr. Ramsey, but if you persist in pressin' this nigger's charge, which, mind you, sir, is still unsubstantiated an' probably will be, because a nigger's a nachral bo'n liar anyway, it'll only result in a lot o' unfriendly feelin' against you, this nigger an' this nigger's folks. An' I know you don't want to hurt his folks."

Ramsey did not answer. The sheriff shook his head again.

"Even if the charge is preferred an' a dead nigger's body is found an' even if you git witnesses you've got to git a coroner's jury to decide it was murder an' not self-defense. An' then you got to git the grand jury to indict. An' even if the coroner's verdict is murder an' the grand jury indicts, which is very doubtful, Mr. Deerin'll have to be tried in this county. How many whites do you figger'll find him guilty? I'm jes' lookin' at all this from the stan'point of arrest an' conviction. There's no use goin' off half-cocked."

"That remains to be seen."

The sheriff spat leisurely.

"Why, there's hardly a white man fit for duty on any o' the juries who don't deal with or work for someone who deals with Mr. Deerin'. A verdict against Mr. Deerin',—an' mind you, sir, I'm even assumin' you git to the trial stage—would upset the whole business life o' the county. How many of 'em dealin' with the Southern Cotton Bank do you figger'll risk havin' their notes called?"

Ramsey's face was expressionless.

"Why, sir, I believe even you deal with the Southern Cotton Bank."

"I have other sources of obtaining money if they call my notes."

"But all this trouble over a nigger," Nichols said disapprovingly.

"There still are some who revolt against the acts of swamp scum!" Ramsey said angrily.

"All I'm tryin' to do is avoid a lot o' trouble," the sheriff said soothingly. "I'm jes' tryin' to point out that it'd be almost impossible to convict Mr. Deerin' or even indict him. You ain' he'pin' the boy. Yo're hurtin' him, him an' his folks. The whites'll git the notion they're gittin' uppity an' take it out on 'em."

136

"Perhaps we can find means to enforce the law."

The sheriff shrugged his shoulders regretfully.

"The law must temper justice with reason. That's why niggers don't vote. If we didn't temper the law with reason we'd have nigger officers, nigger judges, intermarriage, race trouble. No man likes to see murder done, if it was done, an' you can't trust these niggers anyway. They're ready to cook up any charge to git the sympathy of a man like you."

He paused and rubbed his chin thoughtfully.

"I've known Mr. Deerin' since he was a boy. He may show a bad temper when he's mad but he ain't the man to go killin' his he'p. It don't stan' to reason. This boy jes' didn't want to work fo' him an' if you want to git him out o' his contract, why, I figger Mr. Deerin's a reasonable man."

"I gave my word to see this boy safe from Deering's farm and I shall keep it," Ramsey said firmly.

"Well, I'm pretty sure you kin buy'm yo'se'f or maybe Mr. Pearson'll do it."

137

"And let Deering continue murdering his peons?"

"I wouldn't say that. There's no evidence that he did except a runaway nigger's word, a nigger with a chain gang record, too."

Ramsey did not answer. Georgia Crackers were in the saddle, a rising white trash class squeezing wealth from blacks freed from slavery. Crackers had seized the power to vote so they were the law, and by legal trickery had maneuvered the niggers into another bondage. Trash who had lived like slaves were now building mansions on the bent backs of niggers and those whites with contempt for Cracker thievery had to live there, carry on their businesses, raise their families. Protests would mean business pressure, social pressure, community pressure, for most Ochlockonee whites dreamed of riding to riches on the descendants of slaves. The Cracker was riding high, with the law in one hand and the whip in the other. The proclamation to free niggers had really only reduced prices for niggers. White trash who never had a thousand dollars or fifteen hundred dollars to pay for a slave could get niggers now for a

138

few dollars a head by giving them an advance against wages.

Times change and new ways of getting slaves are cunningly devised.

2

A Ford coughed up to the court house. Through the open window they saw Pearson, his face shaded by his hat, walk quickly up the steps.

"What's all this excitement about?" he asked with a wry smile.

"Jes' li'l difficulty," the sheriff said mildly.

"Well, I've heard that Deerin' had trouble with his niggers but it certainly s'prised me that Mr. Ramsey"—he smiled brightly to him —"was talkin' 'bout murder."

Pearson looked at David with a puzzled air.

"I don't know what the hell's happened to this nigger in the las' year. Seemed to be behavin' himself alright befo'."

"Maybe the desire to pick cotton cheaply," Ramsey suggested.

Pearson smiled. Ramsey chewed on a cigar. Pearson stole, too. Some steal with a pistol and some with the law.

139

3

The sheriff looked grave. No one could tell what might be stirred up when a respected citizen like Ramsey wanted to create trouble. These old aristocrats thought they knew how to handle niggers, thought it wiser for the South to keep them contented. Niggers had gone north, a million of them, the papers said, and these whites thought the exodus bad. They wanted to keep them in the South by giving them better treatment and more rights. But many niggers were better off than whites. Whites had to worry about planting, advances, picking and selling cotton, rain. Even a bumper crop did not mean profit. The whole country might have a bumper crop so prices drop, or some outlandish country where workers live on a nickel a day might have a bumper crop and sell cotton cheaper than the South could grow it. Niggers do not have to worry about such things.

4

Ramsey's glance travelled to the worried boy. A nigger in the hands of the whites, the black South, needed for the planting and the reaping and these whites were driving him

140

away. Those two black hands planted the fields and garnered the harvest, built the roads and the mills, raised Georgia from a wilderness. Upon that back the South had built its civilization. There was strength in that nigger, strength to destroy what he carried on his back and these money-grubbing, nigger-trapping whites were too short sighted to see where they were driving him.

"That nigra doesn't know his own strength," he thought.

X

DEERING'S jaws were clenched when he appeared. He nodded to the planters and greeted Nichols with, " Glad you got my nigger, Sheriff."

" There he is, Mr. Deerin', but as I said, there's a li'l difficulty."

" That's alright. I don't expect he'll give me any more trouble."

" Not that way. He's got some kind o' complaint ——"

" Oh, hell! What nigger hasn't? "

Ramsey took the cigar from his mouth.

" In this case," he said gravely, " it's rather serious. This nigra charges you with having committed murder."

Deering's face flushed a brick red. He glanced at David with a hard glint in his eyes.

142

"Well!" he exclaimed. "These niggers will certainly go a long way to avoid paying their debts! Why, Mr. Ramsey, I saved that little bastard from the chain gang and now he says I committed murder. I'll be damned!"

"I do not believe that is his sole reason ——"

Deering's jaws showed white against his skin.

"Are you implying ——"

"I am implying nothing. This nigra is making a grave charge. He tells me he and other nigras are kept locked up under a guard of armed men, that they are terrorized, beaten, and that he saw you shoot a nigra named Limpy Rivers and heard you issue orders to bury the body in a swamp."

"Yes?"

"I was taking him to Atlanta to see the Governor," Ramsey continued blandly, "when the sheriff stopped me with a demand that this boy be kept in the county until he was bailed on the runaway charge. I don't know why he called you or Mr. Pearson but I am here to go his bond."

"I am sure you investigated the charges first?"

"That is up to the authorities."

"And may I ask, sir," Deering said softly, "what business it is of the Governor's unless the machinery of the law has broken down here? Have you complained to the sheriff and has he refused to act?"

"I prefer to deal directly with the Governor, sir," Ramsey returned quietly.

Deering smiled.

"As a taxpayer and a citizen, may I ask why you do not press such charges with the sheriff? If he is remiss in his duties I certainly want to know it. We will have him removed from office."

"I prefer to deal directly with the Governor," Ramsey repeated.

"So. And may I ask"—Deering enunciated the words slowly—"what in hell business this is of yours?"

Ramsey rose to his feet and glared at the planter.

"The business of any decent man tired of seeing nigras robbed, beaten and murdered!"

"I'll see you and this nigger in hell first!" Deering shouted furiously. "I'm sick of this playing anyway! Sheriff, have you any charges against me?"

144

"No, sir, I have not," Nichols said quickly.

"Then I see no reason to continue this farce. I have work to do if Mr. Ramsey hasn't. This nigger has not worked out the advance I gave for him and I'll take him!"

Turning to David he called:

"Come on, you!"

"Just sit where you are, David," Ramsey said quietly.

Deering turned on the white man.

"Ramsey ——" he shouted.

"Mr. Ramsey, sir," the old man reminded him sharply.

"To hell with your misters! Sheriff, that's my nigger and by God! I'm taking him!"

Nichols jumped to his feet.

"Jim! Please! We'll never git anywhere with all this shouting. Mr. Ramsey gave his word to see this nigger out of the county ——"

"I'll see them both in hell first! I'm not going to stand here and see my nigger taken away because he charges me with some cock and bull story! He's a lazy bastard who's already done time on the chain gang and will probably end up by being lynched! I've got his signature to a contract!"

"That boy is not of age and his signature is

145

not worth the paper it's written on," Ramsey interrupted. " But that is not the point. You did not kill a nigra on your farm last week?"

"That's my business! But since you seem to be unhappy without sticking your nose into my affairs, permit me to inform you that I did! And permit me also to add that I'd kill any nigger who comes at me with a knife!"

"You should have reported it, Mr. Deerin'," Nichols said solemnly.

"I called up but you were not in. Then I became busy. I had him buried because the body would stink in that heat. I had planned to notify you the first chance I got and have the coroner hold an inquest. I am ready with my witnesses any time it suits you."

Pearson stirred uneasily in his chair.

Deering glanced at him and smiled.

"Well, now that I've reported it, I must be on my way. Will you be good enough to give me my nigger?"

"This nigra, who you say is lazy," Ramsey said mildly, "cannot be of much use to you. I imagine he would not be very happy going back to your farm now. Would it not be better if you released him?"

146

"I'm not releasing him! That nigger's going to work out his advance!"

"Then I must insist, Sheriff, that you hold this nigra as a material witness in the charges against Mr. Deering."

Nichols shook his head in bewilderment and pulled Deering aside, whispering to him with emphatic shakes of the head.

Ramsey turned to Pearson.

"You want this nigra?" he asked.

Pearson shook his head.

"I reck'n it might cause a li'l trouble ——" he began.

"I understand," Ramsey said icily.

"Mr. Deerin's willin' to let the boy go," Nichols announced.

"If I get my advance back," the planter interrupted. "If you love him so much I'll return him to you for what he's cost me. He's a God damn total loss anyway!"

"Less what he's already earned working," Ramsey suggested. "What is the balance?"

"I don't carry my books with me!"

"Very well, sir. If you will send me a statement of his account with the contract he signed, I'll send you a check for the balance due you."

"I hope everything's settled now, gentlemen, an' that there's no hard feelin's," the sheriff said cheerfully.

Deering turned on his heel and walked out.

"What about the charges?" Nichols smiled.

David looked up pleadingly.

"Please, Mist' Ramsey, I doan wan' tuh mek no charges. I'd lak tuh go wid you, suh, please."

"That's alright, David," he smiled. "I'll take you with me."

2

Ramsey brought the boy to the bus station in the adjoining county seat and gave him ten one dollar bills.

"The Americus bus leaves this afternoon. Take it and transfer there for Macon," he advised. "It has a large nigra population and you can work there. There's a pretty rich nigra there, too, who's good to his race. Maybe he'll help you. I'll see Dee and tell him I saw you out of the county."

The town was like Live Oak, only larger. Concrete sidewalks and wide, concrete streets. Small buildings of brick and dull wood. A

148

drug store on one corner and a general notions store on another. The depot, with its painted signs announcing destinations and fares—Macon, Atlanta, Columbus, Birmingham, Jacksonville.

David peered into the darkened station. Two white women sat on wooden benches, with suit cases in front of them. There did not seem to be a colored waiting room and he stood uncomfortably before the large depot window with another list of destinations and fares painted in bright yellow.

A lean, sun-dried white in a soiled blue shirt approached with a friendly air.

"Lookin' fo' work?"

David was too frightened to answer.

"How'd you like to work fo' me?"

"I cain', suh," the boy choked. "I'm on my way tuh Macon. I'm waitin' fo' de bus, suh."

"All you darkies are always on your way some place," the man snorted and walked on.

There were hours to wait for the bus and the white had scared him. He asked the ticket agent how far it was to Americus.

"If yo' fixin' to walk," the clerk drawled sympathetically, "head yonder till you git to

149

the highway. That'll git you there. Maybe some darkie'll give you a lif'."

Not until he was well in the countryside did he dare ask for a ride. A grizzled old nigger in an empty wagon from which tufts of cotton fluttered, rattled by and David hailed him.

" Goin' far? " he asked timidly.

" Yonder." He nodded vaguely up the road. " Dey's plenty room if you wan' a lif'."

The horse jogged wearily. A wheel careened crazily. The driver wiped his face with a shirt sleeve.

" Goin' far? " he asked.

" Americus."

" Purty far. Whut you gwine dey fo'? "

" Wuk."

" Plenty wuk roun' here."

" I wan' tuh wuk in a mill."

" Ain' no easier'n de fiel's." He glanced sidewise at the boy. " Say, you ain' runnin' away, is you? "

David did not answer.

" Dat's alright. I ain' askin' no questions. Doan you be skeered o' me. Say, if I was to tell 'bout all de niggers I he'ped run away I'd be roasted lak a barbecued pig. Lawd, I've done he'ped mo' niggers run away den dey is

150

on Jake Millet's farm. I ain' askin' no questions but if you is foot-loose you better git outen dis here county. Why, dey ain' a farmer roun' here ain' pullin' de hair out o' his haid worryin' 'bout pickin' dey cotton er shakin' dey pecans er cuttin' dey cane, er jes' plain worryin'."

He wiped his face again.

"Dese white folks ain' happy les' dey's worryin' 'bout somethin'. An' w'en dey starts worryin' foot-loose niggers better start travellin'."

"How far is it to the county line?" David asked anxiously.

"'Bout eight mile. Ain' far. Sheriff Welby's huntin' 'em co'se he gits three dollars fo' ev'ry res' but dat ain' nothin' to git worriet about jes' as long as you is wid me. I got my own farm yonder an' fo' all dey know you's wukkin' fo' me. Git dat worriet look offen yo' face."

Three miles north the nigger came to his cabin.

"Dis is my place," he said. "If you got a dollar er two you'd better tek a bus, boy. Ain' nobody stop you if you got a ticket."

"I got de fare," David said nervously.

" Den you better ride. De Amityville bus passes by here. You kin change dey fo' Americus."

The bus was a luxurious limousine driven by a white in a neat uniform. The fare was collected in advance and David motioned to a seat in the back. There were no other passengers until a white man in overalls, with his coat slung over an arm, hailed the car on the highway. The white man sat with the driver. The front seat was the dividing line for colored and white. Ten miles farther another white standing before his cabin held up a hand and the two whites sat in the back while David sat with the driver.

The Amityville bus station was in a three story hotel. From the ticket agent David learned that the connecting bus did not leave until seven in the morning. He would have to spend the night in town and he started aimlessly for Nigger Town where he could find a lunch counter and a bed but he had not gone two blocks before a stocky white man stopped him.

" Whey you goin', boy? " he asked.

" Americus, suh."

" Whut you doin' in this paht o' town? "

152

"Lookin' fo' de cullud section. I got tuh wait till seven in de mo'nin' fo' de bus."

"Yeah." The white man eyed him meditatively. "Got the fare?"

"Yes, suh."

The boy hastily showed his carefully folded dollar bills.

The man rubbed a two days' growth of beard.

"Live in Americus?"

"No, suh. I live in Ochlockonee county, suh."

"Got relations in Americus?" the man persisted.

"No, suh, no. I ain' got no relations dey."

"Den whut you goin' there fo'?"

"I'm goin' lookin' fo' wuk," the boy explained nervously.

"Oh. No work whey you come f'um?"

"Yes, suh. No, suh," he stammered.

"Whey you fixin' to sleep this ev'nin'?"

David twisted his hat nervously in his hands.

"I doan know, suh. I figgered maybe ———"

"Yeah," said the man decisively. "You figgered. But I figgers I doan lak to see

153

darkies wanderin' roun' loose in this here town in de ev'nin'. Better come along with me."

" Mistuh, I ain' wanderin' roun' loose. I'm jes' lookin' fo' a place tuh eat an' sleep till de bus leaves ——"

" Yeah. I'll give you a place to eat an' sleep. Come along."

" You ain' de law? " David asked miserably.

" Yeah. I'm de law an' I doan lak no vagrants roun' here."

" I ain' no vagrant, Cap'n. I got eight dollars an' I'm on my way tuh Americus. Please doan lock me up. I never hu't nobody an' I'll git out o' here dis ev'nin' if you let me go."

" Come along," the law said bruskly, taking him by the arm.

3

In the small cell in the county jail David's bitterness surged in a rebellious hate that startled even him. He shouted furiously, banged on the iron door, cried and cursed.

A voice several cells away shouted:

" Whut's de matter wif you, nigger? You gone out o' yo' haid? "

4

When the justice of the peace solemnly imposed a fine for vagrancy on him the boy kept his eyes on the wooden floor of the court room.

A white farmer approached with a grin.

" I need a li'l he'p out on my place," he said amiably, " an' I'll advance you the fine if you'll come an' work it off. Pay you twenty-five dollars a month."

David did not answer.

" Whut say, boy? " The sheriff poked his shoulders. " Hit's a lot better'n workin' it off on de roads."

" I ain' goin' tuh sign nothin'," David said sullenly.

" Make him sign! " the farmer exclaimed angrily. " These damn niggers ———"

" Can't make him sign," the sheriff laughed. " It's against the law. This buck mus' a-worked fo' a farmer befo'! "

His belly shook with laughter.

" I don't want him after the second pickin'," the planter protested.

" Tell it to him," the sheriff grinned. " There's plenty work in this county. We kin use'm. We're short o' convicts anyway to finish the road to Jeff Beacon's place."

XI

NIGGERS hired for county work must be paid wages but Georgia Cracker law can hire them for fat back, peas and corn pone.

The weazened justice of the peace, with the unshaved face seemingly swollen from a mouthful of tobacco, peering through silver rimmed spectacles. The corners of the court's mouth, brown and moist where the juice dribbled. The stuttering justice whining:

"T-t-ten dollars an' costs or three months on the ch-chain gang."

The routine for the record was observed to the letter.

In the absence of a clerk of the court the justice sent a certified copy of the sentence to the warden at Buzzard's Roost, Chickasaw county's convict camp, and the boy was re-
156

turned to his cell until the warden or a deputy claimed him.

2

Bill Twine was a huge man, six feet three and weighing more than two hundred pounds. A paunch that threatened to burst from the belt around it swayed like congealed jelly when he walked. A three days' growth of beard made his heavy jowls seem as dirty as his white cotton pants and soiled, white shirt.

"You'll be treated better'n you ever was at home if yo're a good nigger," he smiled to David. His teeth were stained a yellowish brown from snuff dipping. "Good food—all you kin eat. Eat it myself sometime. Guards eat it, too. Three months ain't so much. You'll work out soon an' if you've bin a good nigger you'll git an outfit when you go, same's a state convict."

The boy did not raise his eyes.

"Three months ain't such a long time," the warden repeated. He motioned the boy into the parked car.

Bill Twine did not manacle the prisoner sitting beside him, for short-time convicts do not risk longer sentences by attempting to escape. The boy was silent, morose, answering only in monosyllables when asked a direct question.

On the open road the sunlight, the level, white fields of cotton, the very highway wandering off to freedom snapped something in the boy's brain and without fully realizing what he did he flung the door of the car open and jumped. He struck the road with terrific impact and rolled over and over before he came to a stop and lay crumpled and unconscious at the furrowed edge of a field.

The Ford stopped with a screech of brakes even before David's body had stopped rolling.

"Crazy son of a bitch," the warden muttered, jumping out of the car.

The boy's face, and hands instinctively thrown out to break the fall, were lacerated and bleeding. His clothes were ripped as though a beast had clawed them.

Bill Twine slapped him vigorously until he moaned and opened his eyes.

"Git up an' see if you broke any o' yo' God damned bones," the warden growled.

David rose slowly to his feet.

"Stretch yo'se'f!"

The boy obeyed dazedly and as suddenly as he had jumped from the car, the bleeding hands and face and flapping overalls rushed madly for the open fields.

" Halt! " Twine shouted, pulling a pistol. " Halt! Or I'll shoot! "

As quickly as the insane notion to run had come, the sharp command brought him to his senses and he stopped. Bitter tears were running down his cheeks when he returned at the warden's command.

Twine advanced to meet him.

" So that's the kind o' nigger you are, eh? " He struck the boy with a fist, knocking him to the ground. Blood from his nose formed a scarlet rivulet down his chin.

A car appeared on the road and at the warden's upraised hand stopped. The driver was a nigger who looked sympathetically at the boy in the road.

" Got a rope? "

" Yes, suh." He quickly found a rope under his seat.

" Bind his hands and feet. Put yo' hands out! " he called harshly to David.

The boy put his hands out, but at the touch of the rope to his wrists, stared wildly about

159

him and with a loud cry pushed the nigger
back with a powerful shove.

"You little black bastard!" Twine swore.
"I ought to blow yo' God damned brains
out!"

He raised his pistol and struck David on the
head. The boy dropped without a whimper.
Blood ran down his forehead to his closed eyes
and mingled with the rivulet from his nose.

3

He regained consciousness in the county
jail. His whole body ached. The blood on
his face and hands had dried and the slightest
movement made it crack and bleed again.

There was a patch of bright, blue sky
through the barred window. A sense of help-
lessness and despair swept over him and he
cried with long, deep sobs.

He was in jail a week before a deputy
escorted him to the sheriff's office. His face
was covered with the scabs of healing wounds.

"Tried to escape, eh?"

David nodded dully.

"I reck'n we kin save you some time by
bringin' you befo' the co't now, if you plead
guilty," said the sheriff.

160

David nodded again.

This time the stuttering justice of the peace appointed a lawyer to defend the accused. The lawyer borrowed the prosecuting attorney's plug of tobacco and suggested that it would be wiser to charge the boy with a misdemeanor instead of a felony.

" Defendant is entitled to consideration fo' pleadin' guilty," his attorney drawled. " If you charge him with a felony you'll have to bind him over to a higher co't. He's savin' the county the expense o' feedin' him. In addition, Chickasaw county has mo' felony convicts than its population warrants. If defendant is charged with a felony the county will not profit from his work. He will be transferred by the Prison Commission to another county an' all we'll have is the expense o' keepin' him. I figger it would be wise if the co't kept him here on a misdemeanor charge."

The lawyer smiled cheerfully to David.

" I reck'n that'll save you some time, boy, eh? What say? "

" Hit doan mek no diff'runce whut I say. I'm gontuh git sen' up anyway."

David did not understand the phrases the justice stuttered between wiping tobacco juice from his chin and exploring his nostrils with a long, bony finger. He understood only that for trying to escape he was to do nine months more after he had finished the original three.

4

Misdemeanor offenders may not be sentenced to more than twelve months and are kept within the county of sentence, but felony convicts are the state's and are allotted to counties in proportion to their population. The Prison Commission which has sole control over the state's convict camps consists of three men elected by popular vote. It is not essential that commissioners be penologists but it is essential that they be good vote getters.

Convict camp wardens are appointed by the Commission, upon recommendation of the commissioners of the county where the camp is located, unless the proposed man has too unsavory a record.

The Prison Commission makes its own rules for the supervision of convicts which are subject to no one for approval.

5

A nigger doing life and a year arrived for

the Chickasaw county camp the day David was sentenced. The two were handcuffed together. Ebenezer Bassett was his name and he was in his forties. He had escaped several months before from a northern county camp where he was doing life for having killed a nigger in a brawl. He was caught when he was arrested in an easy house for striking the madame over the head with a chair. He was given a year for escaping.

All this he chattered while they waited under the watchful eyes of a guard while Bill Twine shopped in town for his wife. Ebenezer's face was wreathed in smiles when he talked except in moments when his eyes clouded with a perplexed, bewildered expression; then he looked as though he were groping for something he did not quite understand or grasp.

"Figger you'll escape again, Ben?" the guard asked jocularly.

"Dunno, suh," he chuckled. "Sho got a long time to figger hit out!"

He turned to the boy.

"Whut you doin'?" he asked.

"Year," David said sullenly.

" I wouldn't even hang my hat up fo' dat!
Me—I got life an' a year! "

He laughed loudly.

" Dat jedge is outer his haid! How he
figger a man kin do life an' a year? W'en yo'
daid you cain' do no mo' time! "

He noticed David look at him with a puzzled air.

" Got my haid cracked," he explained
cheerfully. " Skull busted wide open an'
brains jes' ploppin' all over de place."

He shook his head vaguely and added:

" I git awful haidaches sometimes."

He broke into another loud laugh.

" Yes, suh, cracked my skull clean open. I
laid in jail fo' weeks fo' I was up an' aroun'."

The guard watched tolerantly with an
amused grin.

" Jes' one thing troublin' me," Ebenezer
said confidentially, his eyes clouded with that
searching, groping look. " I dunno whey my
wife an' chillun is. Dunno whose gonter tek
care o' dem."

He shook his head sadly.

" Two li'l chillun," he explained, holding
up two fingers of his free hand.

164

XII

THREE of the Buzzard's Roost eight acres were inclosed with barbed wire strung on posts ten feet apart. Beyond the inclosure the ground sloped gently to a green wall of swamp trees.

A wooden cross for the lanterns at night faced two cages in the stockade, huge cages with worn, wooden steps at each leading to the doors open like the maws of iron monsters. There were no pans under them, old cages, where the night's receptacles were kept inside. The criss-crossed, half-inch bars on the sides were screenless. A kitchen of blistered, gray planks sagged on brick stilts half buried in the red clay. Its walls were stained with the years' accumulation of grease until the very boards seemed to ooze of the pots and pans inside. Twenty feet away was the mess hall, as blistered and as gray as the kitchen. A deputy's shack leaned towards two trusties' shacks. In the easternmost corner of the stockade, under planks resting eaves-like on eight posts, was the last stopping place of the convict before free legs were riveted with chains: the blacksmith shop. The shelter was filled with old shovels and picks, chains, broken halters, saws, files, bolts and nuts and old automobile wheel rims.

Two hundred yards from the stockade gate was the warden's house, a slat-board, rambling building with an ancient coat of paint peeling off its walls. A luxurious flower garden faced the ugliness of the wire inclosure. Two acres of vegetable garden, pig and chicken pens stretched back of the house. On these acres were the kennels for the dogs, the terror of convicts and the despair of those who had been tracked down by them.

A heavy, summer stillness hung over the camp.

A trusty came out with two suits of stripes.

" Git in 'em," the deputy ordered.

The change made David resentful. Ebenezer was sobered by the wrinkled convict suit

166

that marked him so irrevocably as of the chain gang until his dying day.

From the open door of a cage a gaunt, black, scarecrow of a man came haltingly down the steps. He was bareheaded and barefooted. His striped pants were rolled above his ankles, and his torn undershirt clung to his bony shoulders. He walked slowly to them.

" Y'all got a lemon fo' a sick cullud man? " he asked plaintively.

They stared at him. The guard laughed.

" No, they ain't got no lemons, George," he said.

The scarecrow returned dejectedly to the cage and sat on the steps, resting his head on his hands.

" He's always askin' fo' a lemon," the guard grinned. " Tried to escape a couple o' years ago an' got pretty badly beat up an' he's bin off since. Good worker, though."

He scratched a stubble of red beard.

" Make yo'se'f to home. Cap'n's gone to the house to register you in his hotel book an' it'll be a while befo' the blacksmith's back."

2

Buzzard's Roost: red clay under a tropic

sun. A cage for niggers and a cage for whites. Flies. Mosquitoes. Tiny red ants. A cross. Two concrete poles eight feet apart and stocks, like a heavy wooden box with three sides missing. To David who had seen men faint in them in Snake Fork, the four holes in the wood were round eyes of terror. And a coffin of thick wood standing upright, the like of which he had never seen, but it was recognizable from the tales he had heard in the convict camp, of men in it who had pleaded for a merciful bullet to end their agony and of one who had died: the sweat box.

The blacksmith came and looked curiously at them.

" Joe," the guard called, " double shacks fo' this nigger," nodding toward Bassett, " an' spikes fo' the other. You first! " he shouted to David.

Sam Gates, the hulking killer in Snake Fork, had had spikes. Twenty pounds of steel bayonets riveted around the ankles. Ten inches of steel in front and ten inches behind so the convict can hardly walk without tripping, or sleep without waking when he turns.

David sat on the ground and held first one foot and then the other on a block of wood

168

while the spikes were being riveted. The eye between the two steel prongs fitted closely around the ankle, with just enough space for pants to be pulled through when changing clothes. The weight on his feet was heavy when he rose. With his first step the projections clashed noisily against each other.

"Spread yo' laigs," the blacksmith cautioned.

David gained the steps of the nigger cage walking straddle-legged. Spikes was the warden's answer to his mad effort to run away, steel to remind him at each step that he was marked for special attention, sharp points of steel, bayonets of steel before him and bayonets of steel behind him—because Chickasaw county wanted to finish a road for a white planter.

3

David and Ebenezer waited on the steps of the cage for the return of the road crews and the call to supper. The two lanterns on the outstretched arms of the cross were sickly in the twilight. The cook's shadow moved fantastically over the small, square panes of the kitchen window. The advancing night covered the squalor of the stockade. The bright green of the hickories and dogwoods, white oaks and bays at the swamp's edge became a deep, purple wall standing jealous guard over its stagnant pools.

A brooding peace settled over this world fenced in by barbed wire.

The older nigger stared moodily at the cross and cracked the knuckles of his fingers.

"I got chillun," he said sadly. "Two li'l chillun—some place."

4

Trucks clattered on the road to Buzzard's Roost. A trusty standing with the warden at the stockade gate lighted two flare torches. Bill Twine leaned his large bulk against a gate post, his heavy face red in the spluttering light.

A guard, steadying his holster with a hand, jumped lightly to the ground from one truck, and taking one of the torches, stood at the gate post facing the warden. The shotgun guard walked twenty feet away and loaded the gun he had unloaded when returning with the crews.

Bill Twine raised his voice:

"Come on, you! Come by me! Lemme smell you! Come by me! Lemme smell you!"

Black and white, chains clanging like an anvil chorus as they struck the earth, clambered out of the trucks and in an irregular file started through the gate. As they passed they counted:

"One."

"Two."

"Three."

Their faces glistened with sweat. Each man paused before the warden who bent forward jerkily and sniffed at their bodies to be certain that the smell of sweat showed a full day's work.

Seven whites and eighteen niggers, most of them shackled; but only one walked with legs spread apart, the spikes catching the torch light like a clean bayonet. Twice he had tried to escape and twice the hounds had found him.

"Fourteen."

"Fifteen."

And over their tired count sounded the warden's monotonous cry:

"Come by me! Lemme smell you! Come by me! Lemme smell you!"

The walking-boss—he with the pistol—ordered one nigger with a thin, harried face to step aside. When the count ended Bill Twine demanded:

" What the hell's the matter with that son of a bitch? "

" Impudent! " the guard returned sourly. " Gi' me as wicked a look as you ever saw when I tol' him to move fas'. Should a-broke his damn black neck right then," he added savagely.

" Cap'n, I didn't ——"

" Stocks! One hour! An' no supper! " the warden snapped. " I don't want no impudence in my gangs! When yo're tol' to move —move! "

When the sweat rolls down your body and the clothes cling to it as though water had been poured over you, and the dust of a Georgia road gets in your nose and eyes and ears and covers you with a reddish film while you shovel fourteen times to the minute, minute after minute, hour after hour,—it's then that you go mad. You forget to keep your eyes on the ground when the guard curses you and say, " Yes, sir," and in your madness you talk back or show the hate in your eyes. Then

172

it means punishment when you return to camp.

The nigger unconsciously rubbed his wrists as a man about to be hanged rubs his throat before his arms are strapped to his sides. He walked between the warden and the guard to the stocks and sat on a flat board lying across the low supports. Bill Twine pulled an iron lever and the boards opened, leaving curved spaces for the hands and feet.

" Put 'em in! "

The convict raised both feet at right angles from his body and placed his ankles in the hollows. His chains rattled against the wood. The warden threw the lever that locked hollows in the upper board over those in which the ankles rested. Wrists followed in the other grooves and the topmost board clamped over them.

With a quick jerk the guard pulled the board from under the imprisoned convict. The body sagged to within three inches of the ground. His weight seemed to tear his shoulders from their sockets. The boards pressed tightly against the arteries of his wrists.

The convict uttered a low, " Oh, Jesus! "

They extinguished the torch and walked away.

The cook cried:

"Come on y'all! Come an' git hit! Come an' git hit!"

The chained things resting on the cool soil of the stockade rose and straggled to the mess hall.

5

It is hard to walk into a cage again.

It was dark and hot inside. He clambered to the upper bunk he was assigned, careful to avoid jabbing the others with his spikes, and stretched out on the blanket crumpled on the straw mattress. It was too much trouble to slip the pants through the eye of the spikes and he removed only his coat and shoes. They all slept in their pants, stripped to the waist, if they had no underwear.

The iron door grated and clanged shut and the noises of the cage at night began: chains clinking, mattresses rustling, a convict humming softly to himself, sporadic comments, curses in undertones, sharp slaps at flies and mosquitoes.

Not a breath of air stirred.

The cage filled with the acrid stench of eighteen unwashed bodies.

174

A nigger scratched himself under the arm-pits. Another belched gas and laughed.

From the adjoining cage a white swore querulously:

" God damn stinkin' niggers! "

6

Through the bars you saw the guard and a trusty go to the shadowy mass in stocks and raise the topmost board. The wrists were released and the convict fell back, his shoulders striking the earth and his legs pointing absurdly upward. When the ankles were freed his feet slid over the board, the chain scraping the wood.

They dragged him like a sack of potatoes to the cage. The door grated again. Those who were not asleep raised themselves on elbows and stared as the trusty lugged him to a lower bunk.

The door closed again. The padlock snapped. Insects droned. Bodies tossed restlessly. A nigger snored. A convict stumbled to the pots.

A wild thing cried in the swamps, a sharp cry of anger or hunger or loneliness.

XIII

IT is hard to sleep the first night in a cage
in the heat and stench, and doubly hard
when legs are weighted with spikes. When
David did sleep he awoke each time he tried
to turn. Once the convict who had been in
stocks startled him from a fitful doze by a
cry of pain felt in a nightmare, and once
the boy awoke from a dream where, lost in a
dismal swamp, his spiked legs were tangled in
twining roots that drew him down into a
glassy, stagnant pool.

It was quiet and peaceful in his father's
cabin now. The half moon was over the
broken chimney and the stars were winking
like silly nigger gals. The sagging front porch
was piled with picked cotton. Zebulon was
asleep with his mouth open, hugging his

176

skinny little arms close to his breast. And over everything was the stillness preceding dawn.

The cook and his helper stumbled sleepily to the kitchen. A lamp was lit and their figures bobbed fantastically on the yellow squares of window panes. The sharp cracks of kindling snapped in two were like distant pistol shots.

The guard sat on the kitchen steps, scratching his neck and yawning.

The cage door swung open and the guard called the old, familiar: " Ev'rybody up! Gittin' out! Shake yo' laigs now! "

Chains rattled and clanged and convicts stumbled sleepily from their bunks, crowding and jostling one another in the narrow aisle.

2

Buzzard's Roost was rushing work on the road to Jeff Beacon's acres. Last year the planter had acquired unbroken land cheaply and the county was now making an ancient cowpath as wide and level as other Georgia roads. An excavator ploughed the soil and convict crews shovelled it into mule wagons that took the load to level deep hollows. In a semicircle about the wagon, their legs planted firmly in the broken earth, they waited for the signal from the walking-boss.

The guard approached David:

" Ever work on the shovel gang? "

" Yes, suh."

Smallpox Carter set the lick for David's crew, a huge, pockmarked nigger doing twenty years for manslaughter.

" Bettah put'm neah me, Boss," he suggested. " Jes' to see dat he doan hu't hisse'f none."

The walking-boss nodded. Convicts must shovel in unison, for if one rises while another bends, an arm may be badly gashed.

The eastern sky turned gray.

" Le's go! " the guard shouted.

Smallpox bent his broad back and with a grunted " Hep! " rose with a shovelful of earth and heaved it into the wagon. As he bent each man in the crew bent with him and when he rose, they rose with him. Steadily, with rhythmic precision, fourteen shovelsful to the minute, they bent and rose to Smallpox's lead. Their breath came in pants, sweat broke out on their bodies. The nigger who had been punished threw his shoulders back after every heave as though to ease a strain on his back.

178

Only when the wagon was full and ready to give place to an empty one, did Smallpox utter a loud " Hol' hit! " and everyone paused, resting on their shovels while the loaded wagon creaked away and the other took its place.

The twenty-pound spikes pulled David ankle deep in the loose earth. The large brogans the commissary had given him filled with soil. His heart pounded. Muscles ached. The red dust settled in his nostrils and mouth. His throat felt dry and when he spat he spat cotton.

In a momentary breathing space while wagons were being changed Smallpox whispered to David:

" Lick too fas'? "

" I'll mek hit," he said doggedly.

The filled wagon lurched. The driver struck the mule's flanks sharply with the long reins.

" Go on, mule! " he shouted.

" Reck'n we'll hit up a slow tune," Smallpox said with a wink.

David nodded gratefully. The huge nigger's deep voice started a rhythmic chant, like the cry of his savage ancestors praying to

179

their gods in the jungle.   As his shovel sank
into the earth he sang:

Uh, uh, Lawd—

With perfect synchronization each shovel
sank into the soil at the last word.

I wonder why—

Eleven shovels swished their loads into the
wagon.

I got to live
Fo' de bye an' bye.

Silence followed the last word.   Shovels
rasped into the soil again in the rest.

De sweet bye an' bye!

As he finished the verse he heaved.

Uh, uh, Lawd,
Doan You bother me.
I'se never happy,
Cept on a spree —

Cain' You see?

Uh, uh, Lawd—
Uh, uh, Lawd—
Uh, uh, Lawd—
Uh, uh, Lawd—

Po' me!

Smallpox's pitted face shone with perspiration though the sun had scarcely topped the wooded horizon. Backs bent and rose in silence. The cries of the driver to his mule sounded shrill.

They sang the same song again. The walking-boss strolled over and listened.

"Hey!" he shouted. "Whut you singin', Smallpox? A lullaby? Wan' to put 'em all to sleep on the job? Better hit up *If I Kin Git to Georgia Line!* It's a lot livelier!"

The huge nigger grinned.

"Yas, sah," he returned without pausing, "but wukkin' faster, Boss, ain' gonter bring mah twenty years roun' no soonah!"

"Well, don't make 'em all lullabies," he cautioned gruffly.

3

If you are young and have been in a chain gang before you know what it means when a strong convict offers you friendship.

There was the Snake Fork cook who had been on chain gangs for fifteen years in different counties who was comforted by a fifteen-year-old boy doing three months, whom the warden gave him as a helper. And when the meal truck arrived and the walking-boss shouted, "Lay 'em down! Come on now, an' git yo' feed!" and Smallpox sat with David, he remembered that Dee had said that to sleep with a man was as evil in the eyes of the Lord as sleeping with a beast of the field, and turned to the lick leader.

"Whut you speckin', Mistuh?" he asked coldly.

Smallpox looked surprised.

"What's de mattah?" he demanded, frowning.

"Lissen," David said quietly, "I bin on a chain gang befo'."

"Tough, eh?"

"Lissen, Mistuh, doan start nothin' wid me ——"

The other convicts sat up at the prospect of a fight. The shotgun guard turned in their direction, sensing trouble.

Smallpox spat contemptuously and walked away.

The boy took his plate of peas and pork and corn pone and sat on the cool, upturned earth with the others. He was wet with perspiration. His body ached. The spikes irritated his ankles and he stretched his feet sidewise to ease the strain.

During the afternoon, when his eyes smarted from the sweat that rolled down his face, he cried to the guard:

" Gittin' out! "

It was the call of the convict camp when a prisoner had to care for nature's needs. He had learned in Snake Fork how convicts use it for a two minute rest when they feel they are about to drop from exhaustion.

" Gittin' out there! " the guard agreed, pointing to low brush on the edge of a field.

4

On Saturday afternoons some bathed in a large pan, less for cleanliness than for the cool feel of water and when they washed five or six used the same pan, for the pump was in the warden's yard and it was too much trouble to carry water for each man. Sometimes the commissary gave them a yellow bar of soap but there were no towels and bodies dried in the sun. Many did not even bathe on Saturdays for it was too long to wait their turn, or because their bodies would be more odorous for the nightly smelling.

David watched a strapping nigger with an open sore the size of a dime on his left leg bathe in water already used.

" Syph'lis," the bather volunteered indifferently, noting the boy's look. " Ah tol' de Cap'n 'bout hit w'en I fus' come an' Dr. Blaine, he come an' looked me ovah an' said hit was syph'lis but he couldn't affohd to buy me no injections an' de Cap'n said he couldn't affohd to sen' a strong niggah away w'en he was shy o' convicts. But hit doan hu't. Ain' no bother a-tall. Hit'll go 'way in a li'l while.

" Yeah. De doctor say ' Whut de hell do you think I am? Come out heah an' spen' mo' money on gas an' oil den de county pays me an' den speck me to pay fo' injections fo' syph'letic niggahs? Hit'll cost a couple o' dollahs a treatment ev'ry week fo' a long time an' if I staht wid dis one, whey I come off at? Ev'ry damn niggah got syph'lis one way or another, anyway. Transfer him if you want to git rid o' him!' "

Chickasaw county paid the county physician

184

one hundred dollars a month, which was supposed to include service, travelling expense
and medicine for the county's sick.

5

But Buzzard's Roost was an idyllic camp
when you heard of others.

Skillet Jones who had spent half. of his fifty
years in camps from the Carolinas to Louisiana said so, told them they did not know a
good camp when they saw it.

Skillet looked as though southern suns had
dried him until there was nothing left but a
parched brown skin stretched tightly over
small bones, and two close set eyes darting
furtively in cadaverous sockets. A long scar
ran from his forehead to his nose, hit with a
skillet by a wench, he explained with a wide
grin.

There was the day David sat near him during the dinner period. Water had spilled
from a pail and the wet clay was a deeper,
darker red.

"Nigger blood," Skillet said viciously.
"All dese roads is red. All through de souf.
So much nigger blood in 'em dat no rain kin
ever wash 'em clean again."

185

He liked to tell stories, talking in his quick, explosive way and interspersing the tales with high cackles of amusement. When a convict, exhausted by the grind, swore sullenly under his breath, Skillet would snicker contemptuously.

"Huh," he would say, spitting disgustedly. "Whut you niggers belly-achin' fo'? You doan know a good camp w'en you see one!"

And he would tell stories of some other gang in some other state.

There was the one when the state of Alabama rented him like it would a mule to a coal operator, and one of the Louisiana swamp where all convicts had malaria but were driven to work with whips while their teeth chattered and their bones ached, and one of the Mississippi camp, where the warden liked to shoot into a gang of niggers to see how fast they could run with chains on their legs ——

Oh, Buzzard's Roost was as clean as an angel's wings and the guards as kind as a white bearded saint to the South Carolina camp from which he had escaped into Georgia. In Buzzard's Roost there were vermin and stench, cursings and beatings and stocks but out of Slatternville seventeen niggers went into the wilderness of the South Carolina hills in a floating cage, a cage drawn by four mules, a swaying, creaking, rumbling prison of thick wood with no bars or windows for air on nights that choked you, and bunks of steel with rings for master chains to lock you in at night. Bedbugs slept with you in that cage and lice nestled in the hair of your body and you scratched until your skin bled and the sores on your body filled with puss. Meat for the floating kitchen wrapped in burlap bags, stinking meat swarming with maggots and flies, and corn pone soaked by fall rains, slashing rains that beat upon the wooden cage through the barred door upon the straw mattresses until they were soggy.

Gaunt-eyed convicts, stinking like foul creatures long buried in forgotten dungeons. . . .

Oh, Buzzard's Roost was a kindly haven to some other camps.

XIV

BUTCH CLYDE was the cook's helper, drove the meal truck when the crews worked a distant road. He had served two and a half of a three-year sentence for stealing foodstuffs from a grocery before he was permitted to drive alone.

On a day when the August sun turned leaves a shrivelled brown and yellow, and convicts and guards coughed from the dust, he drove the truck between the shotgun guard and the shovel-crew. The guard's view was obstructed for a few seconds and he cursed the driver furiously. That night Butch hung in stocks for an hour to remind him never to drive between a guard and his convicts.

At eleven-thirty the next morning when the walking-boss shouted " Lay 'em down ! "
188

Butch had not yet appeared and a mule wagon was sent to look for him in case he was stalled somewhere on the road. They found him under the overturned truck, his right leg broken and complaining of pains in his stomach. They rushed him to camp and in the warden's absence his wife telephoned the county physician while two trusties prepared the cot in a shed reserved for white women visitors when they called on their husbands. A trusty brought a bottle of moonshine from the warden's house and poured a drink down the half-conscious nigger's throat.

Once Butch rolled his eyes in agony, coughed and clutched his abdomen.

"Oh, dat hu'ts," he said with a shiver. "Hit hu'ts. Feels lak mah whole insides is busted loose."

Dr. Blaine came as the warden drew up at the stockade gate. The physician was thin, undersized. His store suit was wrinkled and his nails dirty. He examined the injured nigger and nodded solemnly.

"You'll be alright," he said assuringly. "All you need right now is to set your leg in splints."

He ordered two flat boards, and washing the

189

leg casually, bandaged it. When he finished he said cheerfully:

" I'll send you some medicine. Take a tablespoonful every three hours an' just lay still."

" Cain' you gi' me somethin' to stop de pain, doctor? " Butch pleaded. " Lawd, mah whole stomach feels lak hit's busted loose."

" Yes, yes. I know. The medicine'll stop the pain. You'll have it in a couple o' hours."

The warden walked out with the physician.

" You didn't set his laig ——" he began.

" No. He's got internal injuries an' can't last long. Why torture him settin' his leg? An operation might save him but there's no wing in the county hospital for niggers, an' if you take him to a nigger doctor's house he'll have to stay there for weeks, maybe months. It'll cost the county a lot o' money."

Bill Twine's jowls shook regretfully.

" That's too bad. He was a good nigger. Time almost up, too."

" If you'll send a trusty to town I'll give him something to ease the pain but that nigger'll be gone in a day or two. I'll sign the death certificate now and save myself another trip. Date it the day he dies."

190

"What the hell happened?" the warden asked.

"You heard him," the doctor returned irritably. "Heat. Exhaustion. Dizziness. He didn't git over the stocks last ev'nin' an' when he tried to apply the brakes somethin' went wrong an' the first thing he knew the truck was on him."

"Yeah," said the warden. "Le's sign the papers."

Butch lasted another day. They shipped the body on the milk train to his mother, so the ice would keep it from decomposing before it reached home.

A coroner's jury and the doctor's certificate said Butch was a careless nigger who met an accidental death, but few care how many niggers die of accidents following exhaustion or punishment, nor how many might be saved if permitted into white hospitals.

In some corner of a field lost in a tangle of thicket, a fresh mound marks a Georgia nigger returned by the state to his mother, and a slip of paper is added to the Prison Commission files. A nigger dead of an accident. A nigger dead of disease. A nigger killed trying to escape. Little slips of paper with rubber

191

bands around them gathering dust in Atlanta and little mounds of Georgia clay for mothers to weep on.

2

To Chickasaw county Butch's death meant only one nigger less to work on Jeff Beacon's road and the state would send them another for the county's quota.

The Prison Commission's wheels ground another into the maw of Buzzard's Roost. He came within a week, thin-faced, round-shouldered and with a whipped air. Albert Hope was his name and he was troubled with a cough that shook his body and left him gasping for breath. His papers said he was twenty-one. He had cut a barber with a razor and got ten years for it. The warden of the camp where he had been had asked the Commission to transfer him and the request came in the same mail with Butch's death certificate. The coughing convict was promptly sent to Buzzard's Roost.

When Bill Twine saw the emaciated face and heard the racking cough he swore.

" Jesus Christ! What do they want to sen' niggers like him to me fo'? I can't work that
192

consumptive without killin' him an' I'm not goin' to have my death total raised because some other warden wants his lowered."

He left orders to chain him and put him to work driving a dirt wagon until he could be transferred to the state farm.

"That'll be easy work," he explained.

The convict watched the chains being riveted around his ankles.

"What dey wan' to put dem on me fo'?" he asked plaintively. "I cain' run twenty feet widout coughin' my lungs up."

Two days of work from sunrise to sunset and the nigger coughed up a mouthful of blood. The warden saw him spit it out.

"God damn!" he shouted. "Put him in my car an' I'll take him back to camp befo' he dies on me. Jesus! Why don't they examine 'em before sendin' 'em to a chain gang!"

Bill Twine told the sick nigger to lie in his bunk until the doctor came. The convict covered himself with a blanket though the day was hot. He lay on his back exhausted by spasms of coughing. Sometimes blood welled to his mouth even when he did not cough. Flies gathered on the dark puddle he spat on the floor.

Dr. Blaine did not come. At night a trusty brought a plate of peas and a cup of water to the cage. During the night he had another coughing spell. His head drooped over the bunk and he gasped for air with a peculiar, hissing sound, and spat another mouthful of blood.

Smallpox slipped from his bunk and went to him.

"Do anything fo' you, Con?" he asked sympathetically.

"Jes' a li'l water," he said weakly, wiping the blood from his mouth.

"Cain' git no water now. Have to call the boss-man to open de cage. Hit'd wake de hul camp up."

"Never mine," Con said.

Funny, David thought, lying on his elbow watching them, that of all the convicts the huge nigger doing twenty years, the toughest in the gang, should be the one to offer help.

3

In the morning the guard told Con to stay in bed. Bill Twine brought him a little sugar and condensed milk for his coffee.

When the crews left, the warden took a

194

lantern from the cross and entered the cage. His shadow spread and hovered over the bars and roof.

" How you this mawnin', boy? "

" Pretty bad, Cap'n. Had a bad spell las' ev'nin'."

" Yeah. Well, jes' stay in the cage. When the sun comes up sit in the sunshine fo' a while. That ought to he'p till the doctor comes. I'll have you transferred to the state farm till yo' better."

" Thank-ee, suh," Con said gratefully.

Dr. Blaine did not come that day either. He telephoned he was busy.

" Jes' keep him in bed an' he'll be alright," he said.

When the sun flooded the stockade Con tried to rise but when he moved his mouth filled with blood. But it was easier to breathe with the door open and the pots gone so he did not try to get up again.

The stockade drowsed in its daytime stillness. The trusties were somewhere at work and a silence as of the desert was over everything. Human life was gone; only flies and mosquitoes, red ants and a buzzard flying high across the sun, lived with him.

195

It is terrible to be alone in a dead world
with a dead cross staring bleakly at you but it
is more terrible to be dying alone with chains
on your feet and a buzzard flying high waiting
for your carcass.

4

In the afternoon when Bill Twine returned
Dr. Blaine had not yet come. The warden
swore but Dr. Blaine's appointment was political, too, and there were many reasons why
it was not wise to protest against the county
physician's failure to appear. He it was who
signed sanitation reports. He knew the real
foods fed convicts instead of the foods recorded on paper. Only he could legally state
that a man died of heart trouble or apoplexy
or sunstroke after severe punishment.

The flies rose from the congealing blood on
the floor when the warden entered.

"How you feel now?"

"Pretty bad, Cap'n. Ain' de doctor gonter
come?"

"Sho he'll come. Jes' talked to him. Said
fo' you not to worry none. You'll be settin' a
lively string right soon."

Con's lips spread in a ghastly grin.

196

"No, suh, Cap'n. I reck'n dis is jes' about de en' o' dis here nigger."

The terror in his eyes belied the grin.

The warden grunted and turned to leave.

"Cap'n," Con said quickly as though fearful that he would be left alone before he could utter his request, "do you reck'n I could git a preacher here to me?"

"What's that? A preacher? What the hell do you want with a preacher fo'?"

"Well, suh, I bin studyin' while layin' here in dis bunk dat I never done nothin' much to git to heaven an' I bin figg'rin' maybe a preacher could fix things up fo' me. I'd sho feel better if things was fixed up."

Bill Twine scratched his heavy jowls.

"I ain't figgerin' on you passin' out but if you want a preacher, why I'll git ol' man Gilead down in town fo' you. Sho I'll git him."

"Thank-ee, suh."

"Git'm here in three shakes. Sen' my Ford fo'm right now."

"Thank-ee, suh," Con repeated.

The warden sent a trusty.

"Bring'm back with you," he instructed.

197

"You'll find him in Nigger Town. Anybody'll tell you where he is."

Preacher Gilead came, removing his black, felt hat and bowing respectfully. The white, frizzled hair on his head shone in the sun. He rubbed his straggly, white goatee nervously. His broad, dusty shoes were cracked and his trousers were frayed at the cuffs.

"Young nigra in the cage ast fo' you, Preacher," the warden said amiably.

"Yes, suh. Yes, suh. I'll go dey d'reckly, suh."

For a long time the old man sat crouched on the edge of Con's bunk, just sat and held the boy's thin hand and smiled kindly at him. The insects droned. The sun beat on the iron roof. The sweat ran down his face and the soiled, white collar wrinkled as though trying to mold itself to his throat.

"Never did have no folks since I was no higher'n a barber chair," Con said.

The preacher stroked the boy's hand and smiled gently.

"I bin layin' here studyin', studyin' all de time. Dey ain' nobody to claim my body an' dey'll sen' hit to de students fo' cuttin' up."

The old man's lips moved silently.

"You cain' go fo' de Lawd wid yo' insides all missin' an' yo' haid sawed to pieces."

"I'll ask de Cap'n to let me bury you if you die," the preacher promised gently.

"Will you now, sho?" The boy's face lighted with relief. "I'm scairt, jes' scairt o' bein' cut up. Never be myse'f again—even w'en de angel Gabriel ——"

"I'll go see de Cap'n right dis minute. I'll be back d'reckly."

Bill Twine was directing repairs in the blacksmith shelter when the old man approached.

"Yes, Preacher? How's the boy now?"

"Dat boy's gonter die, suh, I reck'n."

"Oh, I dunno. Dr. Blaine'll be along an' maybe fix'm up good as new."

"Maybe, suh. But dat po' boy's terrible scairt. He ain' got no folks an' he's layin' dey frettin' dat w'en he dies his body'll go to de students fo' cuttin' up."

"Oh!"

"Yes, suh. An' I was figg'rin'," he continued hesitantly, "maybe you could promise him dat he ain' gonter be cut up so's he kin go befo' de Lawd all whole, lak he is."

The warden shook his head.

199

" Hit's the law, Preacher. If they ain't nobody to claim the body fo' burial we gotter sen'
hit to a medical school or bury hit in a pauper's field, an' dey ain' no nigger pauper's field
roun' here."

" Dat boy'd sho die a lot mo' peaceful if he
figgered he'd be buried some place all whole."

" Well," the warden said meditatively, " I
don't know what I kin do."

" Maybe you'd let me bury him, suh—some
place."

" Will yo' burial society take him? "

" No, suh. I reck'n not. He ain' no member. But dey's lot o' lan' ain' bein' used ——"

He motioned vaguely to the sun-baked area
rolling to the swamps beyond the barbed wire.

" I'll tell you what I'll do, Preacher," Bill
Twine said abruptly. " You tell him I'll see
to hit he ain't cut up none. Maybe hit kin be
arranged. That's the bes' I kin do."

" Thank you, suh," the preacher murmured.

" Ain' nothin' to worry yo' haid about, boy,"
he assured Con gently. " Dey ain' gonter sen'
you to de students if you die. Cap'n Twine
jes' promised me."

" I was scairt," the boy whispered. "Awful
scairt."

200

5

A heavy humidity hung over the stockade.

Few could sleep in the heat, and the stench of their bodies and night pots made it hard to breathe. They were wet, sticky as though hot, slimy water had been poured over them.

David was stripped to the waist. The pants clung to his legs, irritating them, and the spikes were monstrous things that grew out of him and were part of him now. His ankles hurt from the rubbing weight and he feared the irritation would bring shackle poison. Sam Gates had had shackle poison and he remembered how swollen the leg was. Sometimes, a convict's leg has to be cut off if the swelling gets too bad.

Smallpox bent his massive form over the edge of the bunk.

" How you, Con? " he asked.

" Not so good."

" Dat doctor man'll fix you up fine," the nigger said cheerfully.

" He'll be a li'l late w'en he do come."

There was something terrifying in the quiet, resigned answer. A nigger cursed. Others raised themselves on their elbows, shadowy forms staring sympathetically.

" I'm alright.   Only I git scairt sometimes,"
the boy said apologetically.

" Hell, dey ain' nothin' to be scairt of! Cain'
nobody git in here to hu't you! Lawd, you
sho pertected in dis cage!"

" No, I'm scairt ev'rybody'll go to sleep an'
leave me alone."

The huge nigger dropped from his bunk,
his chain rattling on the floor.

" I'll set up wid you.   Hell, I cain' sleep
nohow."

He crouched at the foot of Con's bunk.

" Wan' a song, boy, jes' to kine o' cheer you
up?" he asked.

" Dat'd be fine," the boy said.

Smallpox began:

> *If you wanter sneeze,*
> *Tell you whut ter do—*

" Sing *Star in de East,* will you, Smallpox?" Con interrupted.

The huge nigger hesitated.

" Sho, if dat's whut you wan'," he agreed.

" O Lawd," he sang:

O Lawd! Ain' dey no rest fo' de weary one?

One star in de east,
One star in de west,
An' between de two dey ain' never no rest.

Let us cross over de river,
Let us cross over de river,
Let us cross over de river,
An' rest.

O Lawd! Ain' dey no rest fo' de weary one?

Ebenezer Bassett was the first to join in the singing. One by one the others added their voices and those who did not know the words hummed the tune. The whites in their cage listened. The guard came out of his shack and listened.

They sang for an hour, and silence again descended over the cage.

The lanterns on the cross smoked.

Con was asleep, one hand hanging limply over the edge of his bunk.

Smallpox crawled stealthily back to his.

XV

A LOUD cry of terror shattered the silence of Buzzard's Roost. The convicts awoke with starts. A half-naked nigger stood trembling in the passageway, his teeth chattering audibly.

"Oh, Lawd!" he cried. "He's daid!"

A convict swore. A white cried out irritably. Trusties in tattered underwear appeared at their shack door. The guard ran to the cage shouting:

"Hush! God damn you! What the hell's the matter in there!"

"He's daid!" the nigger cried again.

A convict cursed angrily. A voice added a rebellious cry and then another. It seemed that they had been waiting for something like that frightened shriek in the darkness to loosen the floods of their emotions. The cages filled

204

with cries and shouts and bitter oaths. The guard bellowed for them to quiet but his voice was lost in the rising bedlam. White and black, the convicts went mad in a delirium of expression. Cat-calls mingled with screams and curses. Some found their shoes and banged on the iron doors or hammered on the bars. The noise could be heard half a mile away.

Bill Twine, pistol in hand, came running in his underwear, swearing luridly. His paunch wabbled furiously and his jowls shook.

"Git 'im out o' here!" a voice cried from the nigger cage.

"Stop that noise!" the warden roared. "Stop it, or I'll stretch every damn one o' you!"

Timid ones, fearful of punishment, ceased their cries. Others, fearful of being singled out by their voices, stopped. Only an under-current of whispers and indistinct, muttered protests sounded in the nigger cage.

"Git some torches an' open that door!" the warden ordered angrily.

Two bright flares burst hissing and sputtering, throwing a weird light on the frightened faces peering through the bars.

The night guard swung the door open.

"Pile out! All o' you!" he shouted.

They came, barefooted, half-naked and huddled together in front of the cage, silent and apprehensive.

"What the hell happened?" Bill Twine demanded.

No one answered.

"Who started this? Talk now, God damn you! or I'll stretch y'all!"

"I got scairt, Cap'n," the nigger who had uttered the first cry said, his teeth chattering. "He's daid in dey!"

A rush of words came as though he feared being stopped before he explained why he had shrieked. He had started for a pot. Con's hand hung over the rim of his bunk. While bending to avoid an outstretched foot from an upper bunk his chest brushed the hand. It was cold, and the horror of being locked in with the dead had terrified him.

"So that's it, eh? That's why you woke the camp an' raised all this hell!"

"I didn't mean to start all dat, suh. I was scairt. Dey'll be niggers dyin' here'bouts now."

206

" I dunno 'bout the dyin' but there'll be a nigger stretched for startin' this! "

" Please, suh, Cap'n—I didn't mean to start nothin'. I was jes' scairt slapped to death, suh ——"

" We'll see if we kin scare you enough to keep yo' damn mouth shut in the future," the warden returned viciously. " Jesse, git the cuffs an' ropes! "

The night guard handed the torch to a trusty and disappeared into his shack.

" Bartow! Sam! Git that nigger out o' the cage an' put 'im in the blacksmith shelter."

The two convicts carried the dead boy from the cage.

" You stay here! " Bill Twine ordered the still trembling nigger. " The rest o' you git back in there an' don't let me hear any mo' o' that God damned noise. The nex' time I'll stretch ev'ry one o' you! "

Ebenezer approached Twine.

" Cap'n, please, suh," he pleaded, " cain' you put a couple o' pennies on Con's eyes so's he won't look at us w'en we's sleepin'? "

Twine's fists clenched, but there had been enough trouble without terrifying the niggers more, and he growled:

207

"Alright. I'll have a couple o' coppers put on 'em."

Ebenezer scraped gratefully. The night guard came with a pair of shiny handcuffs, snapped them on the nigger's wrists and tied a long rope to the links between the cuffs.

"Come on!" he said, yanking the rope.

Ebenezer turned to the warden again.

"Cap'n, 'scuse me, please, suh, but ain' you gonter have somebody set up wid Con? He'll ha'nt us sho if he ain' waked, suh."

"Alright. You set up with 'im if you want to ——"

"Yes, suh. Be glad to, suh. An' kin I git some salt an' ashes f'um de cook fo' his sickness, too, suh?"

"Yeah," Twine said, and walked to the stunted concrete post to which the guard was already tying the convict.

2

Through the bars figures could be seen moving silently and swiftly before the white post. The warden, an absurd figure in his underwear, held a flare high.

The unresisting nigger, with his back to the post, was laced to it from ankles to hips with a rope and the one tied to the cuffs slipped about the second post. The guard pulled sharply. The convict's torso jerked forward, bending at right angles, his arms outstretched. His head drooped between the arms. The sweat on his back and arms glistened in the light.

"Stretch!" the warden ordered harshly.

The guard pulled until the rope was as taut as a tuned violin string.

"Oh Jesus!" the nigger screamed. "Yo' pullin' my arms out!"

The rope was wound around the post and tied, leaving the convict stretched so the slightest movement threatened to wrench his shoulders from their sockets.

"One hour!" the warden said curtly and extinguished the torch.

Over the moans of the nigger on the rack sounded Ebenezer's low cries. He was a vague shadow rocking on his haunches, waking the dead while arranging the plateful of ashes and salt under the body covered with burlap bags. His voice was indistinct but as his emotions rose it came clear:

"Po' Con!

Po' black boy!

You done lef' us.

No mo' cage. No mo' chains.

No mo' cough an' no mo' blood.

Come on, Consumption, an' git into dat salt an' ashes an' leave dis po' black boy alone!

Leave'm alone so's he kin enter de bright gates o' heaven all good an' whole.

Po' black boy!

Yo' free now ——

Lak a red breast flyin' in de sky. . . ."

From somewhere in the recesses of his memory rose an old lullaby he had crooned to his children:

> *Ol' cow, ol' cow,*
> *Whey is yo' calf?*
> *Way down yonder in de meadow!*
> *De buzzards an' de flies*
> *A-pickin' out its eyes—*
> *Oh, de po' li'l thing cried 'Mammy!'*

"Jesus Christ!" a voice from the white cage shouted. "Can't somebody hush that nigger!"

3

Bill Twine kept his promise not to send Con's body to be cut up by students.

When the convict crews left he picked a secluded spot where tall pines rose against the cloudless sky and the land sloped to the first shallow pool of the swamps, and ordered Ebenezer and a trusty to dig a grave behind a cluster of bushes. Rich foliage shaded the exposed roots of ancient trees in the stagnant water and beyond, the green tangles brooded with its mystery. The dew was still wet on the sparse grass and the morning chorus of red birds were starting their daily hymn to the rising sun.

Four buzzards sailed effortless over the stockade and perched on a dogwood to watch the digging-men. A white butterfly settled upon the fresh turned soil, fluttered its wings, and flew off.

That night, when the cage door closed on them, Ebenezer told the story of Con's burial.

4

A convict who has been stretched cannot work the next day and the nigger was on the cage steps with his head resting on his chest when the doctor finally arrived.

"Is that nigger why you called me so urgently?" he asked the warden irritably.

"No!" Bill Twine returned coldly. "I called you about that T. B. nigger you didn't have time to see. Well, you kin see'm now—under that pile o' bags yonder!"

Dr. Blaine shrugged his shoulders.

"Too bad," he said regretfully. "Have you made out the death certificate?"

"What'll I make it out fo'? That he got consumption since he came here an' died in a few days? I ain't fixin' fo' mo' trouble than I already got. You had no business lettin' that nigger stay in camp! You should have examined him when I first called you last week an' ordered him transferred to the state farm!"

"What's the difference what he died of?" the doctor said in a conciliatory tone. "I'm the one who decides on the cause, so you have nothing to worry about. He died o' heart failure. Most o' these niggers are syphilitic anyway an' they can die of a syphilitic heart as easily as T. B. You're gittin' too upset."

"Too damn many heart failures out o' this camp."

"Oh, hell, make it anything you want!" he exclaimed testily.

Bill Twine filled out the report. For cause

212

of death he wrote laboriously: " Just dropped dead."

" That's good enough," said Dr. Blaine.

" There's no claim on this body an' he was scared o' bein' cut up by students an' I promised to have him buried. He was a good nigger an' it ain't his fault he's dead."

" Sure. You can't ship the body anyway. Damn thing'll decompose by the time it gets anywhere. An' you won't make the county sore by taking him off its hands."

5

A trusty brought Preacher Gilead. His white hair seemed a little thinner than before when he removed his hat in the warden's presence and bowed gravely.

" Mawnin', Preacher," the warden said. " That boy—he's dead, you know."

" Yes, suh," he said tonelessly. He glanced at the nigger on the cage steps and sighed.

" I promised not to turn him over to the students so I'm havin' him buried on the premises. I figgered you'd want to hol' services."

" Yes, suh."

" Body's by the grave yonder."

"Yes, suh, I'll go d'reckly."

Soil lay on one side of the deep, red hole and the burlap-covered Con on the other.

The preacher uttered a startled "Oh Lawd!" when he saw the grave.

"Y'all done digged dat no'th an' souf—right at de cross-ways o' de worl'!" he said reproachfully. "How dat boy tu'n roun' w'en de golden trumpet soun's an' de daid begin to git ready to git up out o' dey graves?"

The convicts looked frightened, and worried lest they have to dig another grave east and west.

Red ants scurried under the bags as though unable to wait until the body was laid away. More buzzards flocked to the dogwood and sat motionless, eying them with cocked heads.

The old man shook his head. In a loud voice he cried:

"Chillun! Look on de face o' yo' brudder!"

"My brudder in de arms o' Gawd," Ebenezer crooned. He raised a bag from the face. Two copper pennies lay on the closed eyelids.

Tears rose to Preacher Gilead's eyes. He wept as he pocketed the coppers.

214

"He's done worked out his time an' he's a free sperit now," he said gently.

"Lak a bird in de top-mos' pine," Ebenezer crooned.

The convicts lowered Con into the grave. The plateful of salt and ashes, with ants crawling over it, lay dull in the sunlight.

"Ashes to ashes," the preacher mumbled, scattering them over the bags. The trusties shovelled the soil into the grave. The old man raised his head and clasped his hands together fervently:

"O Lawd, Who got kindness an' mussy in Yo' heart fo' all things,

Dis boy's a-goin' home—

Flyin' lak a mockin' bird straight to You.

Spread Yo' white wings over him.

Mek him fo'git dey was chains on his feet

Lak You made Yo' people fo'git dey was slaves w'en You tuk 'em outer ancient Egypt.

Great is Yo' mussy. Hit endureth fo'ever—

Sho, sho, You got some fo' a po' cullud boy."

He looked so old and shrivelled standing there, with the veins in his hands showing and the raised chin so scraggly and drawn.

Ebenezer and the trusty shovelled steadily,

215

eying each other and the preacher suspiciously lest one dash for the stockade to avoid being the last to leave the six-foot graveyard and thus be the next to die. Their quick breathing and worried looks were so pronounced that the old man stopped abruptly. Ebenezer paused, fearful lest they fly before they even filled the grave and leave him to struggle as best he could with his chain.

A look of deep compassion spread over the preacher's face.

"I'm a ol' man," he said gently, "an' hit doan matter much if de Lawd calls me, so y'all jes' tek yo' time. I'll wait right here till you is gone."

When the last pats of the shovels smoothed the mound he said quietly:

"Y'all kin go now."

XVI

"SHO. Bury 'em in swamps," a voice said. "Who cares? Yo' nothin' but a nigger."

"Should a-taken care o' dat boy," said another. "Hit ain' right to let 'em die lak dat."

"Niggers got no rights. Mules got rights. Mules cost money," the first voice said bitterly.

"Should a-taken care o' dat boy," a third voice said with deep conviction. "Prison Commission sez dey gotter tek care o' you if you's sick."

"Yeah. Prison Commission sez de doctor gotter be here w'en dey punish you, too."

"Somebody oughter write 'em 'bout dis boy."

"Yeah? An' dey'll sen' a inspector an' he'll

repo't Con got de bes' treatment. De Cap'n an' de doctor'll say de same. An' w'en dat's over you'll wish you was out dey wid Con."

" Yeah. Nothin' to do 'cept wuk out yo' time—or die out."

" Or run out."

" An' git ketched an' put in de sweat box."

" Lots o' convicts run out."

" Yeah. Whey? Tell me dat? Whey dey run? "

" Houn' dogs on lan' an' wild cats in de swamps."

" Yeah. Dey ain' no 'scape fo' niggers."

2

But even to think of escape makes it easier when the guard curses and the sweat dribbles down your body while you bend and rise, bend and rise, fourteen shovelsful to the minute, hour after hour under a tropic sun. Shackles are off and a free body runs in the fields, in the swamps, on the highway, hunted by man and dogs but—free.

In the noon period Ebenezer dropped tiredly beside David at the roadside and stared morosely at the spikes.

" I got de blues," he said.

The boy nodded sympathetically.

" I'd lak ter see my two chillun but I doan even know whey dey is."

David did not answer.

" I could fine 'em if I was out."

The sun's glare hurt the boy's eyes and he covered them with his hat. The guard and the walking-boss sat with their backs to a tree, watching the convicts.

Mules grazed on the seared grass.

" I foun' 'em once w'en I run out an' I kin do hit again."

" You got tuh run out fus'."

" Dey oughter be two w'en you run out— one to watch w'en de other's sleepin'."

David turned on his side to look at him. Ebenezer's eyes were bright.

" Ain' no use. You'd git ketched an' beat half tuh death."

" Not if I meks de swamps at night. I know swamps. I lived in 'em till I was man-size. Dey ain' nobody kin fine me in a swamp in de dark. Nobody. Not even a houn' dog. An' by sunup I'd be whey dey couldn't fine me even in daytime."

" Yeah? Yo' big trouble is mekkin' de swamps."

"I got dat all figgered out."

The boy raised himself on an elbow to look with startled interest at him.

"I got a steel file—f'um de blacksmith shelter."

"Whey yo' got hit?" the boy breathed excitedly.

"In de brush near de grave. Threw hit in w'en we was carryin' Con dey."

"How you figg'rin' mekkin' de swamps fo' de guard shoots you?" David asked eagerly.

"Dey cain' shoot you in de ev'nin'. Dey cain' even see you. Gimme ten minutes an' dey'll never fine me. Houn' dogs ain' no good in swamps if you sticks to water."

David shook his head.

"How you git ten minutes start?"

"Dat's whut I got all figgered out," Ebenezer said triumphantly. "Jes' a li'l mo'nin' on Con's grave."

It was a simple scheme and in its very simplicity lay the chance for success. The warden knew the nigger custom of mourning the dead and decorating graves with broken crockery, cans, pots—anything sufficiently useless not to be stolen. As for the closeness to the swamps, everyone in Buzzard's Roost

220

knew enough not to try for them. Two had fled there once and two weeks later a trapper had found what the wild cats had left of them. The warden would have no fear of a break in that direction, not with chains and spikes on their legs. Only the open road held hope for escaping convicts in this camp, and on that the hounds would find them.

Against capture and punishment was the chance of success, of shedding spikes, and the fear of shackle poison that might cost him a leg and leave him a helpless cripple, unfit even for a white man's farm.

The thoughts raced through his mind. To the excited imagination the escape was an accomplished thing.

"W'en you fixin' tuh try?" he asked eagerly.

"Dis ev'nin'. Right after supper," Ebenezer said.

3

The afternoon was long.

To David the work songs to which he shovelled merely heralded an approaching freedom. Even the guard's customary cries and curses fell on indifferent ears.

The sun sank behind the fields and the guard shouted " Lay 'em down! " In the truck Ebenezer sat at his side and while the car shook its way through the gloom, pressed his foot gently, a friendly pressure. Bill Twine called " Come by me! Lemme smell you! " under the reddish flares. In the mess hall the older nigger caught his eye with a significant look that made his heart pound fiercely.

He was half through with his supper when Ebenezer got up.

David knew what to do. He had been told in a few swift sentences and he raised his legs over the bench and followed him into the yard. The boy walked slowly to the kitchen. He saw the warden and the night guard talking together but they did not look at him.

The cook raised his head from the pots and pans.

" You got somethin' I kin put on Con's grave? " David asked hesitantly.

" I reck'n so." His large, flat nostrils quivered. He took two broken pitchers and a dented pan from a shelf and gave them to him.

" Too bad 'bout dat boy," he said sympathetically.

222

"Yeah," said David.

He walked awkwardly towards the warden with the pitchers and pan in his arms. Ebenezer, smoking nearby, strolled towards them casually. David's legs seemed weighted with added steel and a cold sweat broke out when he saw Bill Twine and the guard look at him.

"Please, suh," the boy said timidly, "I got dese f'um de cook, suh, an' I was wond'rin' if I could put 'em on po' Con's grave."

"Hell!" the warden exclaimed. "These damn niggers'll have a grave lookin' like a junk pile in no time!"

Then, with a tolerant shrug of his shoulders, he said:

"Sho, if you'll make it snappy. Near time fo' bed, y'know."

"Yes, suh. Thank-ee, suh," David stammered.

Ebenezer approached, bowing and smirking.

"Kin I go too, suh?" he pleaded. "I was jes' figg'rin' 'bout him all alone out dey ——"

"Ain' you done enough mournin'?" the warden laughed.

He glanced instinctively at the chains and the boy's outspread legs.

"Alright! But make it snappy," he said good-naturedly.

The guard grinned. They watched the two walk slowly to the stockade gate.

"Keeps 'em satisfied," Bill Twine said. "Makes 'em less trouble to keep in line, an' they're safe. A three-year-old kid kin outrun 'em."

Beyond the stockade gate Ebenezer chuckled.

"Lawd! Dat was easy!"

"Yeah," said David excitedly.

It had been so simple. Excluding the first low chuckle of satisfaction neither uttered a sound. At the mound they slipped behind the little cluster of bushes. Not twenty feet away was the first pool of stagnant water and the darkness of the unknown.

The lanterns on the cross were bulbs in the distance and the lighted windows of the mess hall and kitchen, glowing squares of light.

Ebenezer fumbled in the bushes.

"I got hit," he called tensely.

He held the file close to his body. It was a foot long.

David threw the pitchers and pan on the

mound and stood shaking with excitement, staring at the darkness of the swamp's edge.

"Lawd, I cain' go ten feet in dey widout gittin' cotched in dem roots," he whispered. "An' dey I'll be, stuck dey, waitin' fo' de houn's!"

"Dis ain' time ter start yo' worryin', boy. If we ain' back in ten minutes dey'll be huntin' us. Come on! I know dese swamps better'n de stockade!"

With a frightened look at the tranquil, star-drenched land, David slipped after him into the swamp. Water from a pool seeped into his shoes with soothing coolness. A spike caught almost immediately in a tangle of roots and he jerked his leg desperately before he freed himself.

"Put yo' feet careful on dem roots," Ebenezer cautioned nervously. "Feel yo' way. Hit's darker'n a voodoo hell in here!"

Tall trees and intertwined branches heavy with leaves shut out the sky except for scattered patches through which stars shone brightly. David followed blindly, holding on to his companion's coat. Under a cowled cypress was solid ground, some wild creature's path, and he stepped on it with relief. Ebe-

225

nezer heard the firm step and with an irritable mutter pulled him roughly.

" Git offen dat path! " he exclaimed. " You wanter leave a trail fo' dem dogs? Whut's de matter wif you? "

The older convict felt his way with the instinct of a jungle animal. They were wet to the knees. The chains were troublesome and the spikes more so. Once David had to extricate himself by tearing feverishly with his hands at the roots in which it caught. He could scarcely take five steps without the long prongs catching in roots or sinking in the slimy mud.

It seemed to them that they had been in the swamp a long time before the first, faint cry came with the warning that they were missed. The boy plunged forward in a spurt of desperate fear.

" Doan you go to losin' yo' haid now! " Ebenezer exclaimed angrily. " Dey ain' a-comin' through dese here swamps wid no houn' dogs. If dey do dey'll go by de paths."

He moved quickly to a motionless mirror of water over which the sky hung like a lighted dome, and paused to listen.

The smell of rotting fish hung over the

226

water. Frogs croaked. By the starlight they saw that the pool extended several hundred feet, triangle shape. The bank to their left was lined with cypress trees.

" Dis cain' be much deeper," Ebenezer whispered. " Le's mek dem cypress shadows."

They waded through the primeval slime and reached the shadows before the faint baying of the hounds came to them. They heard Bill Twine roar but the words were indistinct. Another and still indistinct cry sounded, followed by shouts and the crash of men plunging into the swamp.

" Dey cain' go far," Ebenezer whispered. " De dogs'll lose de scent an' de Cap'n an' guards ain' got no special likin' fo' wadin' in swamp water an' maybe gittin' bit by a rattlesnake. Dey'll be gittin' back right quick an' hunt us ter-morrer."

The calls of the guards and the weird, frantic baying of the dogs became clearer but the brush and trees and leaves were so dense that they could not even glimpse the torches. Ebenezer whispered encouragingly. If the search reached the pool, they would submerge until only their heads were out of the water; but even while he was whispering the hunt was

227

recalled. The sounds of crashing retreated and the frustrated cries of the dogs told them that the scent was lost.

The stillness of the jungle settled over them. Only the croaking of frogs and the vague noises of the night ruffled the swamp's peace.

With a high, excited chuckle Ebenezer said: "We did hit, eh?"

David laughed nervously.

"Yeah. Now whut we do? How long we have tuh stay here?"

"'Bout a week. Dey'll be huntin' us till den. De fus' thing ter do is git dese shackles off."

They found a clump of thick, intertwined roots, gnarled and bulbous, hanging over the water and sat on them. Ebenezer commenced filing immediately.

"Didn't I tell you," he said. "You stay wid me an' I'll git you outer dis mess, safe on de way ter yo' folks."

"I doan want tuh git back tuh my folks. Dey'll be huntin' me dey."

The older convict's arms moved rhythmically while the file screeched against the steel around his right ankle.

"I doan lak chain gangs nohow," he said.

228

"I want ter fine my two chillun an' git up no'th wid 'em."

When the first shackle fell he uttered a triumphant:

"Dey she is!"

When the second was filed through he let them and the twenty-inch chain drop into the water at his feet, laughing delightedly at the faint ripples.

"Dat's one chain ain' never gonter trouble nobody no mo'," he said grimly.

He gave the boy the file.

"Right here," he said, pointing to the riveted eyes encasing the ankles.

The sultry night turned cool by the time the spikes dropped with a splurge into the water. The boy rubbed the irritated ankles. It was hard to believe that his feet were free again and he stretched and bent them in the sheer joy of free movement.

"Le's travel," Ebenezer said. "We got ter git on as far as we kin fo' daylight. Den we'll sleep, with no trail fo' dem houn' dogs ter pick up."

The dragging weight was gone. Even moving through slimy pools and thick vegetation was a joyous sensation. When a gray patch

229

spread cool over the branches and the red birds commenced their morning song, Ebenezer picked a dry spot under a curtain of low branches and told David to sleep while he watched lest some accident bring the hunters or a trapper upon them.

XVII

IT was high noon when David's sleep was broken to take the watch.

It was cool and shady in the heart of the swamp. Where the sun shone, it was on a primeval world of lush green. A small, luster-less pool, in which floated dead leaves and broken twigs, was at the right and a dense forest of dogwood and maple, hickory and cypress on all sides, shiny moss and thickets of brush and long grass and ferns. Life chattered and chirped but only when a bird flew scold-ing from its nest in a flurry of excitement did leaves tremble, catch the sun and send it shim-mering over the dead water.

Ebenezer snored and turned restlessly. He slept with his mouth open, his legs spread wide in the luxury of space. David stretched lazily, revelling in the sense of freedom. At this hour the convicts of Buzzard's Roost were shovelling soil on Jeff Beacon's road, shovelling fourteen times to the minute, minute after minute, hour after hour while the sun beat upon them and the sweat ran down their bodies and red dust filled their nostrils and open, panting mouths.

Ebenezer awoke with a start.

"Well, how you?" he grinned happily. "Dey ain' foun' no tracks, did dey? Didn't I tell you dey ain' no dog livin' kin fine me in a swamp!"

"Yeah. Nothin' bin roun' here."

"I doan know how big dis swamp is, but we'll jes' keep travellin' souf till we git to hits edge. Mus' be some farms whey we kin fine water."

He led the way again through underbrush and paths tracked by wild creatures. They walked boldly, no longer caring whether leaves rustled or branches snapped, and before the shadows of approaching evening threw a gloomy haze over the swamp they saw a tract of level ground and a dilapidated cabin and barn through a net of cypress leaves. Close by the swamp was a clump of cane

232

planted apparently by the farmer for his own use.

Ebenezer whispered to David to wait while he crept forward, moving stealthily, with the grace of a wild cat stalking its prey and with as much sound. He returned with a broad grin.

" Fo' whites pickin' cotton," he chuckled, " an' no dogs aroun'. W'en hit gits dark we'll fine water an' maybe somethin' to eat."

2

The slender cane brakes rose in a dark mass. They broke two stalks and stripped the bark with their teeth, chewing the pith.

"Wonder who lives dey," Ebenezer said thoughtfully, staring at the two lighted windows of the cabin.

" Whoever hit is, dey know dey's two convicts loose."

" Yeah."

When the cabin lights were extinguished and they were convinced the farmer and his family were asleep they wormed their way around the cane to the first stripped cotton row, gliding cautiously on hands and knees lest their forms silhouetted against the sky tell a

233

waking person of their presence. Near the barn was the mule pen and a watering trough filled with water. They drank in it eagerly.

The barn door was fastened with a stick inserted in two rings. There was a pleasant smell of hay inside. As their eyes grew accustomed to the darkness they searched the walls for overalls and finding none, crept out.

They regained the safety of the swamps and followed its edge until another cabin rose against the sky but a small pen near it made them uncertain whether it was for chickens or dogs and they dared not risk a close inspection. A mile south and another cabin leaned drunkenly against a wide spreading live oak. Ebenezer left to reconnoiter for food and clothes while David waited.

His companion did not return. The boy's anxiety turned to fear and when a cabin window glowed yellow with the warning that farmers were rising he knew Ebenezer had deserted him. He must have found a pair of overalls and had started alone without troubling to say good-bye. Fear lest the convict left his stripes where they could be found for the hounds to smell or that the farmer would learn a pair of overalls had been stolen and

234

notify the sheriff or the warden, terrified him and he retreated into the swamp, wading through pools until, in a bed of thick ferns, he found a dry spot where he stretched out to sleep.

For three days he lived on the mushy fringes of the swamp, always moving north when night fell. There was water to be found in mule pens and once he stumbled across a peanut farm and once he wallowed in luxury in a melon patch. His body was a mass of sores where flies and mosquitoes bit him, and his clothes, torn on brambles and broken branches, were caked with the dried slime and scum of the pools. His face was gaunt from the days of broken sleep, thirst and hunger and fear, and his eyes mirrored a growing despair.

3

He was awakened by hounds baying. In a terrified glance he saw Bill Twine's huge form, a guard and two trusties holding dogs straining at their leashes, and the scared faces of a nigger and his family. The boy retreated into the swamp, stumbling in his haste. The sound of his flight brought wild shouts from

235

the guard and fierce cries from the hounds. The guard crashed after him, swearing luridly as he sank in a pool. The unleashed dogs leaped through the brush in a mad desire to reach him. The shotgun roared and snipped leaves and twigs from low branches.

With a helpless little cry the boy stopped, shaking and trembling. The dogs leaped about his ragged, terrible figure with triumphant cries. The guard, dripping with water and cursing furiously, reached him and without a word struck him in the mouth. Bill Twine appeared, panting, his paunch swaying.

" Got 'im, eh? " he called. " Carry 'im out! "

He snapped handcuffs on the boy.

" Ought to blow yo' God damned haid off fo' all this trouble," he swore.

The niggers, with their cotton sacks hanging from their shoulders, stared sympathetically when they came into the open field.

" So yo' goin' to dec'rate Con's grave, eh? " the warden said viciously. " Put one over on me, eh? You an' that smart lifer! Don't like my gang, I guess. Well, that's jes' too bad. Yeah, too bad. We'll try to make yo' stay with us a li'l mo' pleasant from now on."

236

4

Ebenezer was in the stockade. David saw him lying near the stocks in the blaze of sun, trussed up like a pig ready for slaughter. His head lay loosely on the red soil as though the neck had been broken. His eyes were closed. His legs and arms, tied with ropes, pointed to the sky, the whole body kept motionless by a pick thrust between the tied limbs. His mouth was open. The veins in his temples and arms stood out, swollen. And swarming over the face and arms and neck were myriads of tiny red ants.

Bill Twine paused at Ebenezer's form and rolled him over with a foot.

" Let'm rest fo' an hour," he instructed the guard, " an' restrict'm again. We'll see how he likes bein' free!"

While the guard removed the pick from between bent legs and arms the warden marched David to the sweat box.

" You got a lot o' dirt on you," he growled. " Nothin' like a good sweat to git it off you."

The terrified boy turned a haggard face to him.

" Please, suh," he pleaded, " kin I git a li'l water, fus'? "

" Sure." The warden waved a magnanimous hand. " There's the swamps. Lots o' water. He'p yo'se'f any time you feel like it."

The thick door of the pine box was opened and he was thrust in. The padlock snapped.

It was dark inside except for a small spot of light entering a two by four inch air hole in the top. The box was too narrow to turn around in and he stood motionless, a living mummy in an upright coffin. The tropic sun beat upon it. Sweat dribbled down his face and body. His tongue was dry, thick, swollen. It was hard to breathe.

He heard Bill Twine's muffled order to pour water over Ebenezer.

He became dizzy. He opened his mouth for air. The dried swamp filth and slime on his body and clothes dissolved and ran down his chest and legs. The striped suit clung to him. His wrists expanded from the heat, swelled, and the handcuffs chafed and irritated them. His head ached. A mosquito entered through the air hole and fastened on his neck despite his spasmodic jerks to dislodge it. Flies whirred and droned about his head.

He heard the warden order Ebenezer trussed up again. The nigger pleaded, his words indistinct.

Sometime in the afternoon he could no longer restrain the demands of his bowels and bladder and his excretions dribbled down his thighs.

The humid, stifling air in the sweat box filled with a sickening stench. Flies and mosquitoes, attracted by the odor, swarmed through the air hole.

A merciful blanket of unconsciousness covered him.

He was awakened once by Ebenezer's sobs:

"Oh, please, please, suh. I cain' stan' hit no mo'."

5

He heard the convict crews return and Bill Twine crying:

"Come by me! Lemme smell you! Come by me! Lemme smell you!"

The cook cried:

"Come an' git hit!"

The sweat box was opened in the morning. The boy fell out, unconscious, bloated, swollen.

239

6

When he regained consciousness he was lying naked on a lower bunk in the cage. The handcuffs and stinking clothes had been taken off and a blanket thrown over him. The door was open. It was broad daylight and the somnolent hush of the day was over Buzzard's Roost.

A tin cup of water lay on the floor beside him and he drank it, his hands shaking.

Ebenezer was across the narrow tier staring pityingly at him.

" Dey stretched me," he said weakly. " Dey stretched me till I tol' 'em whey I lef' you."

David did not answer.

" I got spikes now." He raised a foot to show the pointed, steel prongs.

David turned his face to the bars.

In the afternoon he was given a suit of stripes. A trusty helped him to the blacksmith shelter and spikes were again riveted around his ankles. Bill Twine snapped an iron collar with a padlock and a five-foot chain around his neck and jerked the boy back to the cage. The loose end of the collar chain, long enough to reach the pots, was locked to the criss-crossed bars.

240

From his bunk he could see the tiny red ants scurrying in all directions and the shadow of the cross dark on the red soil.

APPENDIX I

Illustrations

The Prison Commission of Georgia

E. L. RAINEY, Chairman
G. A. JOHNS, Vice-Chairman
VIVIAN STANLEY, Commissioner

ROOMS 315-317 STATE CAPITOL

ATLANTA, GA.

IDA Z. HENDERSON
SECRETARY

PHONE: WALNUT 2120

September 24th, 1930.

To All Wardens:

This will introduce Mr. John L.
Spivak, who is making a study of convict
camps in Georgia. Please extend to him
all co-operation and courtesy.

Very truly yours,

Vivian Stanley

Commissioner.

The Prison Commission of Georgia

E. L. RAINEY, Chairman
G. A. JOHNS, Vice Chairman
VIVIAN STANLEY, Commissioner

ROOMS 415-411 STATE CAPITOL

ATLANTA, GA.

IDA J. HENDERSON
SECRETARY
PHONE: WALNUT 2120

October 20th, 1931.

TO ALL WARDENS:

      This will introduce Mr. John L. Spivak, who is making a study of convict camps in Georgia. Kindly extend to him all co-operation and courtesies.

      Very truly yours,

      Vivian Stanley

      C o m m i s s i o n e r.

"One star in de east,
One star in de west,
An' between de two dey ain' neber no rest."

Convicts working in unison by singing. Rhythmic movement
is necessary to avoid injuring one another while bending or
rising

......Clyde......, Ga., Aug 23, 192*0*

County......Bryan......

To The Prison Commission of Georgia,
Atlanta, Ga.

Gentlemen:

I report to you this day the following:

Jack Bones al Jack Barnes
Prisoner's Name

Chatham
County Where Convicted

Dec. 14, 1939
Date Received in Penitentiary

Dec. 14, 1939
Date Received in This Camp

Burglary
Crime

= - 3 yrs
Sentence

INSTRUCTIONS.

7. _Chatham_
Received From

BODY OF CONVICT
FOUND IN RIVER

Apparently drowned while trying to swim the Ogeechee river, the body of a negro convict was found near King's Perry yesterday morning about 11 o'clock. There was a shackle on the right leg. County policeman D. T. Downing made an investigation and learned that the negro had escaped from a Bryan county chaingang recently. Identity of the drowned man could not be ascertained immediately.

Dr. G. H. Johnson, Chatham county coroner, viewed the body and released it to an undertaker for burial.

escapes, recaptures, discharges, **p a r o l e s a n d deaths must be reported promptly the day they occur.**

8.
Transferred From

9.
Transferred To

10. _Aug 18 1930_
Escaped

11.
Recaptured

12.
Discharged

13.
Paroled

DESCRIPTION WHEN RECEIVED:

Black Color	_17_ Age	_male_ Sex	_160 lbs_ Weight
_5ft 8in_ Height	_Black_ Color of Eyes	_Black_ Color of Hair	_Light_ Complexion

Physical Condition Authority for Transfer

mother 14 ? York St Savannah Ga
Nearest Relatives and Postoffice Address

Scar over right ear
Scars and Marks and Remarks

This man was found dead aug 20 1930 in the Ogeechee river will forward certified copy of evidence & verdict of coroner jury _Geo. B. Lowery_
Name of Warden

A BOY TRIES TO ESCAPE

A HALTER FOR THE NECK

The iron collar chain is locked to the bars of the cage.

Official Punishment Report from Georgia Penitentiary.

Monroe Co. Camp Monroe County,

for the Month of August 19 30

DATE	NAME OF CONVICT	CAUSE AND PUNISHMENT
aug. 19	Bud L. McCoy	Chains for talking back to guard.
aug. 20	Bud L. McCoy	In stock 40 minutes for refusing to work.
aug. 4	Joe Lay	Stripes & placed under the "gun" for cutting up at side-camp
aug. 29	Saxon Woodard	Double-shackles for fighting on job
aug. 29	Jonas Jackson	Double-shackles for fighting on job.
aug. 29	J. C. Roberson	Extra heavy chains for fighting on job

The above is a correct list of convicts who have been punished at said Camp for the month of August 30

(Sign Here) O. M. Clements
Deputy Warden.

AN OFFICIAL REPORT FROM MONROE COUNTY

THE CAGE

where convicts are herded like beasts of the jungle. The pan under it is the toilet receptacle. The stench from it hangs like a pall over the whole area. Flies and mosquitoes feed on the pan's contents and then enter the cage through the holes in the screen

TEARING AT THE LEASH

A white and a black trusty chaining camp bloodhounds to
trail two escaped convicts

H. M. FULLILOVE, M. D.
SURGERY GYNECOLOGY
AND OBSTETRICS

G. O. WHELCHEL, M. D.
MEDICINE

St. Mary's Hospital, Inc.
Athens, Georgia

MISS JEWELL HARALSON
SUPERINTENDENT

June 1?, 1931.

Sec. of Prison Commission,

Atlanta, Ga.

Dear Sir:

    ... colored, felony convict in ... County prison
died of apoplexy Saturday afternoon. ... sick about four hours.

    Yours truly,

    H. M. [signature]
    County Clerk

A CONVICT DIES—

Athens _____ Ga. June 13,1931 _192____

County_____ Clarke _____

To the Prison Commission of Georgia,
Atlanta, Ga.

Gentlemen:

I report to you this day the following:

1 _Will Harris_____ 2 _Clarke_____
    Prisoner's Name   County Where Convicted

3 _Oct. 25,1930_____ 4 _Oct. 25, 1930_____
    Date Received in Penitentiary   Date Received in This Camp

5 _____Burglary_____ 6 ____1 to 2 yrs_____
         Crime   Sentence

INSTRUCTIONS. READ CAREFULLY.	
All information required on lines 1 to 6, inclusive, must be furnished in every instance.	7 _____ Received From
	8 _____ Transferred From
If received on commitment use line 7.	9 _____ Transferred To
If transferred from another county, use line 8.	10 _____ Escaped
If transferred to another county, use line 9.	11 _____ Recaptured
Receptions, transfers, escapes, recaptures, discharges, paroles and deaths must be reported promptly the day they occur.	12 _____ Discharged
	13 _____ Paroled

DESCRIPTION WHEN RECEIVED:

Black	40lbs	Male	148 lbs.
Color	Age	Sex	Weight
5 ft.4½ ins.	Black	Black	
Height	Color of Eyes	Color of Hair	Complexion

_____   _____
Physical Condition   Authority for Transfer

_____Winnie Harris, Madison Ave., Athens, Ga.____
         Nearest Relatives and Postoffice Address

__Died with apoplexy at 5 O'clock P.M. June 13,1931__
         Scars and Marks and Remarks

__Dr. H M.Fullilove, attending physician._____

                    R. L. Ester.
                         Name of Warden   M.

OF APOPLEXY

(Note that he became sick during the noon meal period)

June 19th, 1930.

Mr. T. Newell Post
W a r d e n,
Savannah, Ga.

Dear Sir:

We enclose a letter from George Neal a life
prisoner in Chatham County, in which he states that he is
"suffering untold pain and can't get any medicine," that he
is "swelled all over" and that the people there laugh at
him when he asks for medicine.

Please have your camp physician examine him and
write us fully in regard to his physical condition.

Very truly,
THE PRISON COMMISSION OF GEORGIA.

Secretary.

Copy to George Neal
Camp #3,
Savannah, Ga.

A CONVICT COMPLAINED—

DESCRIPTIVE REPORT

From _____ Chatham _____ County.

_____ Savannah ____ Ga., June 24th, 19 30

To the Prison Commission of Georgia,
Atlanta, Ga.:
    I report to you this day the following:

COMMITMENT

Prisoner's name __George Neal.

Alias _____

County where convicted __Wayne .

Date received in the pen. __5/6/27.

Date received in this camp __3/17/30.

Crime __Murder. _____ Sentence __Life.

IF TRANSFERRED FROM ONE COUNTY TO ANOTHER

Transferred from _____Wayne County.

Transferred to _____Chatham County.

Authority for transfer __Prison Commission.

ESCAPE AND RECAPTURE

Escaped __6/16/30. _____ Recaptured ____6/18/30.

DISCHARGE AND PAROLE (Died Ga. Infirmary
                                          6/23/30.

Discharged _____ Paroled _____

DESCRIPTION WHEN RECEIVED

Color __Blk _____ Complexion __Blk.

Age __20 ___ Sex __male ___ Weight __135 ___ Height __5' 6"

Color of eyes __blk _____ Color of hair __blk.

Physical condition __Good

Marks and scars __Enlarged nable, 2 upper teeth missing,
1 tusk upper left, Small scar on top of left wrist.

HAS THIS PRISONER BEEN PREVIOUSLY CONVICTED?

IF SO STATE WHEN AND WHERE

IF MARRIED STATE NAME AND ADDRESS OF WIFE OR HUSBAND

NEAREST RELATIVES OR FRIENDS __Mother, Jennie Robinson,
Scriven , Ga. .

                          _____ Deputy Warden
                                          Chatham County

AND A CONVICT DIED

ORIGINAL
No. Report _____   165

GEORGIA PENITENTIARY
DESCRIPTION LIST

From _Turner Co Farm_ Camp

Ashburn , Ga., 4 - 2 3 , 19 31

Name _John Wesley Kendoll_

Color _Bk_

Age _19_

Crime _Manslaughter_

County _Turner_

Term _10 to 15 yr_

Date Received _Apr. 24 - 26_

Height _6 ft_

Weight _160_

Color Hair _Bk_

Color Eyes _Bk_

Remarks _Died Apr. 25 - 1931_
Accidential death
by the hand of
J. J. Conner.

L. E. Richardson
Warden.

A BOY IS KILLED—BY ACCIDENT!

NORTH'S GARAGE
TELEPHONE NO. 37
ASHBURN, GEORGIA

Georgia,Turner County.

We,the jury selected to hold inquest and hear the evidence touching the death of John Henry Wesley Kendall,find that he came to his death from gun-shot wound at the hards of J.J.Connor and believe that the shooting was accidental.

This the 28th day of April 1931.

_____
Foreman.

List of the jury:

    Ed Walker,
    Mark Rainey,
    N.G.Zorn,
    .R.Whatley,
    D.T.Sumner and
    J.N.Raines.

A JURY AGREES WITH MR. CONNOR

SPIKES

These 20 lb. weights permanently riveted around the legs are a drawn-out torture leading to exhaustion. During the day they rub against the legs, creating sores which often become infected. Such infections are known as "shackle poison." At night the convict's rest is repeatedly broken by the need of raising his legs whenever he turns in his bunk.

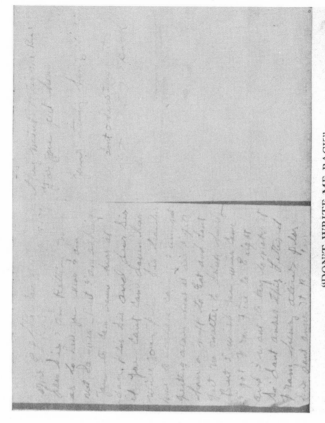

"DON'T WRITE ME BACK"

A convict's scrawl: "ples Sir dont anser it Bee case thay mint Kill me Bee for you geet hear"

Hawkinsville, Ga., 6-16   1930

County Pulaski

To The Prison Commission of Georgia,
Atlanta, Ga.

Gentlemen:

I report to you this day the following:

Charlie Riggins — Troup
Prisoner's Name — *County Where Convicted*

6-16-30
Date Received in Penitentiary — *Date Received in This Camp*

Burg
Crime — *Sentence*

INSTRUCTIONS.
READ CAREFULLY.

All information required on lines 1 to 6, inclusive, must be furnished in every instance.

If received on commitment use line 7.

If transferred from another county, use line 8.

If transferred to another county, use line 9.

Receptions, transfers, escapes, recaptures, discharges, paroles and deaths must be reported promptly the day they occur.

7. Troup Co Jail
Received From

8. _____
Transferred From

9. _____
Transferred To

10. _____
Escaped

11. _____
Recaptured

12. Died 6-20-30
Discharged

13. _____
Paroled

DESCRIPTION WHEN RECEIVED:

Blk — 22 — male — 140
Color — *Age* — *Sex* — *Weight*

5 ft 9 in — Blk — Blk — Blk
Height — *Color of Eyes* — *Color of Hair* — *Complexion*

_____ — _____
Physical Condition — *Authority for Transfer*

Lila Jewell 922 Big Spring Road LaGrange
Nearest Relatives and Postoffice Address

Cut Scar on right elbow
Scars and Marks and Remarks

Shackle Scar on right leg

W. P. Conkle
Name of Warden

AFTER FOUR DAYS IN A CONVICT CAMP—DEATH

Official Punishment Report from Georgia Penitentiary.

_____ Camp, _____ County,

for the Month of _____ 1911.

DATE	NAME OF CONVICT	CAUSE AND PUNISHMENT

STUFFED INTO A BARREL

A variation of the "sweat box"

SICK CONVICTS IN CAGE
Stripped to the waist because of the intense heat.

Official Whipping Report from Georgia Penitentiary.

_____ Camp,   Clarke   County.

for the Month of   August   1930   19

DATE		NAME OF CONVICT	Restricted Hours	CAUSE
Aug.	1	Will Cleveland	1	Fighting
"	1	George Heard	1	Fighting
"	1	Jimmie Mapp	1	Fighting
"	1	Andrew Roseman	1	Fighting
"	5	John Howard	½	Not working
"	5	Eugene Heard	½	Not working
"	5	Clifford Clarke	½	Not working
"	5	Howard Nellis	½	Not working
"	5	Dan Fuller	½	Not working
"	5	James Fleeman	½	Not working
"	5	A.M. Franklin	½	Not working
"	5	Carlton Brittain	½	Not working
"	5	Johnny Cleveland	½	Not working
"	5	Johnnie Harris	½	Not working
"	5	Jimmie Mapp	½	Not working
"	5	Joe Stephens	½	Not working
"	6	Eugene Heard	1	Playing off sick by Dr. Fullilove's orders.
"	6	Crip Brittain	1	Playing off sick by Dr. Fullilove's orders.
"	9	John Howard	1	Not working
"	9	Lucius Cooper	1	Not working
"	9	Joe Stephens	1	Not working
"	12	Robert Willingham	1	Not working
"	12	Walter Jackson	1	Not working
"	12	Crip Brittain	1	Not working
"	12	James Fleeman	1	Not working
"	12	Clifford Clarke	1	Not working
"	13	Johnny Cleveland	1	Not working
"	13	Johnnie Harris	1	Not working
"	13	John Roberson	1	Not working
"	13	W.E. Whitehead	1	Not working
"	13	A.M. Franklin	1	Not working
"	16	Johnnie Oates	1	Cursing
"	16	Lucius Cooper	1	Cursing
"	17	John Howard	1	Cursing
"	17	Andrew Roseman	1	Having dice
"	19	Will Cleveland	1	Impudent talk to guard.
"	19	Horace Smith	1	Fussing
"	19	Johnnie Harris	1	Fussing
"	19	Robert Osborne	1	Fighting
"	19	Walter Jackson	1	Fighting
"	19	Paul Ellis	1	Impudent talk to guard.
"	19	Johnnie Oates	1	Impudent talk to guard
"	19	Robert Osborne	1	Cutting prisoner
"	19	Joe Stephens	1	Disobeying orders of Night Guard
"	26	A.M. Franklin	½	Not working
"	26	Herman Young	½	Not working
"	26	Jennie Young	½	Not working
"	26	James Ferguson	½	Not working
"	26	Jennie Mapp	½	Not working

The above is a correct list of convicts who have been punished by whipping at said Camp for the month of August 1930.

(Sign Here) R. L. Carter
Deputy Warden.

AN OFFICIAL REPORT FROM CLARKE COUNTY

THE DAMNED

"begging for mercy just as we would be at the judgement day"

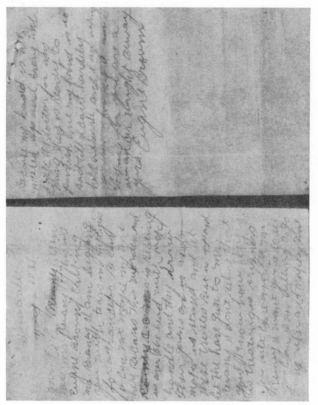

A CONVICT'S LETTER

STOCKS

The convict hangs by wrists and ankles two inches from
the ground. He is left thus under the tropic sun. The
position is an excruciating torture which quickly pro-
duces unconsciousness.

Official Punishment Report from Georgia Penitentiary.

_____ Camp, _____ County.

for the Month of _____ 19_1

DATE	NAME OF CONVICT	CAUSE AND PUNISHMENT
Sep. 5	Ernest _____	_____
" 8	Edgar Miller	Fighting
" 8	Ed Whelan	"
" 8	_____	not working
" 11	Horace Burnett	"
" 11	_____ Worthen	"
" 15	_____	"
" 23	Jeff Smith	Pretending to _____
" 26	_____ Walker	not working
"	Edward _____	"
"	_____ Starling	"
"	George _____	"
"	Ben _____	"
"	Ernest _____	"
"	_____ Daniel	"
"	_____ Warren	"
" 28	_____	Fighting
"	Willie Reid	"
"	J. B. Brimmer	"

The above is a correct list of convicts who have been punished at said Camp for the month of _____

192___

_____ Deputy Warden

AN OFFICIAL REPORT FROM MADISON COUNTY

Athens _____ Ga., Feb. 23, 1931, 192__

County _____ Clarke _____

To the Prison Commission of Georgia,
Atlanta, Ga.

Gentlemen:

  I report to you this day the following:

1 George Johnson _____ 2 Clarke _____
            Prisoner's Name   County Where Convicted

3 Oct. 25, 1930 _____ 4 Oct. 25, 1930 _____
     Date Received in Penitentiary   Date Received in This Camp

5 Larceny from house _____ 6 3 to 5 yrs _____
            Crime   Sentence

INSTRUCTIONS. READ CAREFULLY.	7	Received From
All information required on lines 1 to 6, inclusive, must be furnished in every instance.	8	Transferred From
If received on commitment use line 7.	9	Transferred To
If transferred from another county, use line 8.	10	Escaped
If transferred to another county, use line 9.	11	Recaptured
Receptions, transfers, escapes, recaptures, discharges, paroles and deaths must be reported promptly the day they occur.	12	Discharged
	13	Paroled

DESCRIPTION WHEN RECEIVED:

Brown _____ 27yrs _____ Male _____ 161 lbs
    Color   Age   Sex   Weight

5 ft. 10½ ins. ____ Black _____ Black
    Height   Color of Eyes   Color of Hair   Complexion

_____ _____
Physical Condition   Authority for Transfer

Hattie Johnson, 958 River St., Athens, Ga.
          Nearest Relatives and Postoffice Address

Birth mark on left arm.
          Scars and Marks and Remarks

Has been sick with T.B. for some time. Died

Feb. 23, 1931 3 o'clock A.M. Dr. H.M. Fullilove

attending physician.   R. L. Estes
                              Name of Warden

A MAN WHO BELONGED IN A HOSPITAL DIES IN A
WORKING CAMP

THE GEORGIA RACK

Known as "stretching" and "restricted movement." The convict is laced to a post and the rope tied to the handcuffs is
pulled around the second post until the arms are almost torn
from their sockets. The "stretched" convict is then left under
the broiling sun. They frequently lose consciousness within
an hour

On the Chain Gang

International Publishers issued *On the Chain Gang,* a 1932 pamphlet
in which Spivak described the research that led to the novel.

Preface

These flashes of chain gang life are written by the author of *Georgia Nigger,* the sensational novel about peonage and chain gangs. In this pamphlet Mr. Spivak, a well-known New York newspaper reporter, paints some of the scenes he witnessed in Georgia.

The Georgia chain gangs described here are no different than those found in any other southern state. For the chain gang, with all its brutal forced labor and torture, is a southern institution, adapted specifically to the equally brutal system of peonage in the Black Belt. The plantation owners, credit merchants, and bankers of the South have evolved it as their own peculiar weapon with which to enforce debt slavery and peonage particularly for the Negro peasantry in the Black Belt. It is part of the whole system of repression.

By the use of the vagrancy laws "unattached" or unemployed workers are picked up by the police, thrust into chains, and forced to work either for the county or for planters. There is no distinct line between the two in the Black Belt. In the large plantation areas of the South the sheriff acts as the planter's foreman recruiting and driving labor for him wherever it is required. Objections by Negro croppers to conditions on the plantations receive swift satisfaction—on the chain gang. Working class organizers, Negro and white, have been thrust into chains for leading the revolt against such conditions. The Supreme Court of Georgia has upheld the 20-year chain gang sentence against Angelo Herndon, young Negro organizer who was sentenced, under an old slave insurrection law, for his organizational activities.

During recent years the chain gang has been used more and more for unemployed white workers also. This only proves that as long as the white workers permit the enslavement of the Negro people they themselves suffer much the same fate at the hands of the ruling class.

The special oppression of the Negro toilers exists in the North also. Here the Negro is crowded into Jim-Crow ghettoes, lynched both by mobs and courts, terrorized by the police. He is in fact little freer in the North than in the South.

And both North and South, the Negro workers in industry and on the land are fortunately beginning to move toward revolt against their conditions. The organization of share-croppers unions, as at Camp Hill, Alabama, the active participation of Negroes in recent strikes of coal miners, the wide struggles developing around the Scottsboro case, and the joint fight under the leadership of the International Labor Defense of white and Negro workers against recent frame-ups illustrate the beginnings of these revolts. Together with the white workers, the Negro workers are moving forward toward the abolition of lynching, Jim-Crow laws, and every form of persecution and oppression.

LABOR RESEARCH ASSOCIATION.

ON THE CHAIN GANG

By John L. Spivak

I saw the Spanish Inquisition of 300 years ago. I saw men chained by the neck like galley slaves. I saw men with monstrous bayonets riveted around their feet so they could not sleep without waking when they turned. I saw men trussed up like cattle ready for slaughter and ants crawling over their helpless bodies. I saw men hanging in stocks such as the Puritans used in their crudest days. I saw men broken on the rack as they broke them under the Spanish Inquisition.

I saw these things and I photographed them—not in a forgotten dungeon in ancient Spain but in the United States—in Georgia—in this year of our "civilization" 1932!

"Stretching" on the Early County, Georgia, chain gang,
Warden J. D. Williams supervising. (Photo by John L. Spivak.)

We talked in low tones, sitting there on the two worn, wooden steps of the Seminole County, Georgia, convict camp stockade. The night was heavy, stifling.

The rasping sound of snores disturbed the hush over the wire inclosed world. They came from a huge cage, like one in which a circus pens its most ferocious beasts. Two lanterns hanging on the outstretched arms of a cross driven deep in the soil threw a sickly, yellowish light over the stockade.

In a momentary lull in the chorus of snores the faint sound of rustling could be heard, a sound as of a wild beast creeping through a tangle of jungle brush.

"What is that?" I asked.

"Straw mattresses," the night guard replied. "When they turn in their sleep, you know."

"Yes," I said, "and that clinking sound of iron?"

"The clank of their chains when they turn in their sleep," said the guard.

A mosquito lit on my neck and I slapped at it. A fly droned about our heads.

I strolled over to the cage. A sickening stench rose from a zinc pan under it, used by the prisoners at night. Through the screened bars I saw them stretched out on the iron bunks ranging the cage in three-decker tiers, the whites in a compartment near the door and the Negroes in the rear. Coats and shoes were off. They slept in their trousers, their chests bare, for few had underwear. In the faint light from the cross the sweat on their backs glistened.

One scratched himself tiredly. Another slapped at one of the insects that hummed and buzzed in the cage, insects attracted by the pan under the sleeping men and entering through the holes in the screen. And one, who could not sleep, lay on an elbow looking at me through the bars with despair in his eyes.

"What did these men do to be chained and caged like this?" I asked.

"Anything from vagrancy to murder."

Thirty days and thirty years mingled indiscriminately. There, with his face pressed close to the bars for the cool feel of iron on his hot forehead was a boy who could not have been more than seventeen; and in the bunk adjoining his was a thin, weazened man in his fifties, with a face marked by years of suffering and being hounded.

"A killer," explained the guard.

The cook, sleeping in a sagging, dilapidated shack in a corner of the stockade, was awakened. He came out scratching himself and pulling his jacket over his torn underwear. He stumbled to the kitchen. A lamp was lit and his shadow moved across the dirty window panes like a weird, fantastic bat.

The smell of coffee filled the air.

Tin plates and cups clattered on the long, wooden mess hall tables, shining with the grease of countless meals under the lamp hanging from a beam in the ceiling.

With a harsh, grating sound the iron door of the cage swung open.

"Everybody out!" the guard shouted. "Come an' get it!"

Bare feet thudded to the floor. Twenty-inch chains riveted around their ankles rasped and clanged as they struck the rims of the iron bunks. The convicts straggled sleepily out of the two-foot aisle in the cage and down the wooden steps to the cool soil, a ragged crew, three whites and eight Negroes.

I entered the cage while they were at their breakfast of grits, molasses and coffee. The stench from the pan mingled with the smell of the eleven unwashed bodies which had slept there. Flies and mosquitoes buzzed and droned angrily. The mattresses and blankets were filthy.

A truck appeared at the stockade gate. Streaks of a drab dawn flecked the sky and Seminole County convicts were ready to be taken on the road for their day's work, for the State of Georgia requires that "the hours of labor shall be from sunrise to sunset."

They counted out as they passed through the gate, a straggling, weary crew, their chains dragging on the dark soil.

I talked with a seventeen-year-old Negro boy sitting on the steps of the stockade commissary. There was tragedy in his eyes.

"Tell me," I said, "what did you do to get in here?"

The boy smiled bitterly and shrugged his shoulders.

"A white man wanted a road from his farm finished quick," he said helplessly.

I understood what he meant. I had heard similar stories. Negroes arrested for swearing. Negroes arrested for shooting crap. Negroes arrested for "talking back to a white man." Unemployed Negroes arrested for vagrancy. It did not matter much what excuse was used so long as husky black boys could be arrested and sentenced to the chain gang—to build roads for planters to transport their crops or to press the Negro cropper into debt slavery to a planter. Between slavery on the chain gang and slavery on the plantation there is not much to choose.*

All of the county convict camps in Georgia are run by wardens appointed by the State Prison Commission. The Commission consists of three men elected by popular vote every two years for a term of six years. Their office is in the State Capitol in Atlanta and in a little room cluttered with letters and papers and desks sits Commissioner Vivian E. Stanley.

"How do you rehabilitate your prisoners?" I asked.

"Georgia," said the Commissioner firmly, "takes the attitude that these men committed a crime and consequently owe a debt to society. The State proposes to collect this debt."

So I set out to discover, with a letter of introduction from the Commissioner in my pocket, what the crimes were and how "the state collects its debt."

I went out on the road to watch the Seminole County prisoners work.

I had seen men stripped to the waist before a roaring inferno stoking a ship; I had seen men in steel mills working with molten iron; I had seen men deep in the bowels of the earth cutting coal, but I had never seen a Georgia chain gang at work and I said to myself: "This cannot be so everywhere. I will go to a larger town. This county is lost in rural Georgia. It must be different in other places."

I stood with Warden C. H. Wheatley on a Sumter County road. The road was torn up. Red clay was heaped high in irregular mounds to be shovelled into wagons and transported to level hollows. Convicts in stripes, with their feet shackled, ranged in a semi-circle, ankle deep in the soil, shovelling it into a mule wagon. A Negro set the lick, for a shovel crew must work in unison lest if one digs while another heaves, they slash each other's arms.

The lick leader was a hulking, two hundred-pound convict and he hummed a tune as he shovelled. The convicts bent and rose with him in perfect rhythm. The sun beat upon them with tropic fierceness. Their

*Recent books and pamphlets on present-day Negro slavery published by International Publishers and International Pamphlets include Walter Wilson's *Forced Labor in the United States;* James S. Allen's *The American Negro* and *Negro Liberation;* and *Lynching,* by H. Haywood and M. Howard.

mouths were wide open, gasping for air. Little rivulets of sweat ran down their faces and their striped suits clung to their bodies. The soil dribbled into their shoes as they bent and rose, bent and rose, fourteen times to the minute, minute after minute, hour after hour—from sunrise to sunset under that burning sun.

Dust hung in the air like a cloud, dust that settled in their nostrils and mouths and ears and covered them with a fine, red film.

I left Sumter County wondering if men drop under that terrific strain.

There was that death report in the State Capitol in Atlanta, the one about Will Harris who died of apoplexy in the Clarke County convict camp stockade at five o'clock in the afternoon of June 13, 1931. Dr. H. M. Fullilove, the county physician, said Harris had been sick about four hours. I wondered if working from sunrise to sunset under a burning sun is conducive to apoplexy.

Or George Johnson, who was a strapping youth of 27, five feet ten and a half inches tall and weighing 161 pounds. He had coughed up his lungs on the Georgia highway. "Sick with T.B. for some time," Dr. Fullilove had reported when the boy died at 3 o'clock in the morning of February 23, 1931—of T.B. they said.

I wondered why this youth was kept in the Clarke County stockade until he died if he had T.B. The Prison Commission rules say: "When a convict is found to be permanently impaired or diseased, so as to incapacitate him from labor, the physician shall certify the fact to the Prison Commission."

I wondered if Dr. Fullilove had certified the fact before George Johnson died, and if so, why the ailing convict was not transferred. And I saw that this law had been passed to placate a few harmless reformers and that it was as dead as the laws that were supposed to have freed the Negroes.

I wondered if men and boys go mad under that strain and prefer the silence of death to the agony of the chain gang. Like twenty-year-old George Neal who drank phosphorus, soap and turpentine rather than continue in the Chatham County chain gang. I remembered this boy's letter, a pitiful complaint mailed hopefully to the Prison Commission saying that he was suffering untold pain and couldn't get medicine, that he was swelled all over and that people in the camp laughed at him when he asked for medicine.

The Prison Commission wrote as a matter of form to Warden T. Newell West at Savannah on June 19, 1930, quoting the boy's complaint. Two days later, on June 21, Warden West replied with an equally formal letter from county physician J. C. O'Neill that "He has been so singularly free from anything pointing to such a condition that it must be self-induced by taking substances such as phosphorus, soap and turpentine. . ."

There was nothing said about the boy's complaint that people laugh at him when he asks for medicine. There was nothing said, but two days later they mailed in George Neal's death certificate.

I remembered those death certificates, the neat little batches with rubber bands around them, each telling a story of one dead of apoplexy, tuberculosis, heart failure, sunstroke . . . little sheets of paper in the Prison Commission office where they are neatly filed away and forgotten.

On a wide stretch of highway with the sun shining clear I saw a man working with a group of convicts and as he shovelled the sun caught the glint of bayonets on his feet.

"What are those?" I asked.

"Spikes," said the guard.

Spikes. Long, steel bayonets riveted around ankles, ten inches long, in front of you and ten inches behind, so that when you walk you can scarcely keep from tripping.

"Why those instead of chains?" I asked.

"Reminds them when they wake up in their bunks that it doesn't pay to run away," said the guard. "Every time they turn in their sleep they have to wake and raise their legs."

I remembered Commissioner Stanley telling me:

"We have no spikes in Georgia."

But now I knew better.

I had heard of the sweat box. When I first saw one it was standing in the sun beside a cage. Stood there like an upright coffin, with its long shadow etched on the red soil of the stockade. It was solidly built of unpainted pine and its heavy wooden door was wide open. A revolting stench was over it.

A convict had just been taken out. He lay on a lower bunk in the cage, his eyes closed, moaning. It was two hours before he was able to talk. He told me what had happened from the time the thick door of the pine box was opened and he was thrust in and the padlock snapped shut.

It was dark inside except for a small spot of light entering a two by four inch air hole in the top. The box was too narrow to turn around in and he stood motionless, a living mummy in the upright coffin. The

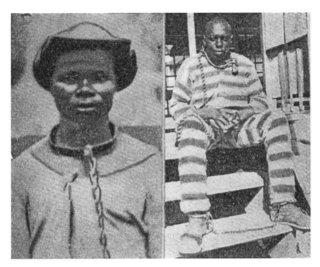

SLAVERY TODAY

IN LIBERIA AFRICA
A native chained by the
neck and forced to work
on the roads

IN GEORGIA, U.S.A.
Chained by the neck in a
Muscogee County chain
gang camp.
Photo by John L. Spivak

tropic sun beat upon it. His tongue was dry, thick, swollen. It was hard to breathe.

He became dizzy. He opened his mouth for air. Perspiration ran down his chest and legs. The striped suit clung to him. His head ached. A mosquito entered through the air hole and fastened on his neck despite his spasmodic jerks to dislodge it. Flies whirred and droned about his head.

Sometime in the afternoon he could no longer restrain the demands of his bowels and bladder and his excretions dribbled down his thighs.

The humid, stifling air in the sweat box filled with a sickening stench. Flies and mosquitoes, attracted by the odor, swarmed through the air hole.

That was all he remembered.

A merciful blanket of unconsciousness had covered him.

A hundred convicts were relaxing in the Muscogee County camp stockade that Sunday morning. As I walked through the white-washed cages the sounds of a hymn reached my ears. Some preacher was leading them in song and while the preacher taught them to pray I found a convict lying on a bunk with an iron collar locked around his neck, like some ancient galley slave.

"He ran away," said the Warden.

"I want to talk to him alone," I said, and the warden withdrew.

"Why did they do that to you ?" I asked.

He looked sullenly on the ground.

"You may talk freely," I said. "There will be no harm come to you for it."

"Not while you are here," he said.

"What happens when no outsiders are here?" I persisted.

"We get hit over the head with sticks and pick handles," he said.

Prison Commission rules—such a pretty cloak for the Georgia inquisition!—said: "Guards shall not be permitted to strike a convict except to prevent escape, in his own defense or in that of another, and in no case will be permitted to curse a convict." And I remembered prison inspector S. W. Thornton's letter on May 16, 1931, from Milledgeville to Miss Ida J. Henderson, the Commission's secretary:

"I expect that one of the commissioners did have an axe handle and did use it which in my opinion was the best way to get them out of the cage."

And I remembered the Prison Commission's letter (for the newspapers and for the records) to Mr. Thornton on July 30, 1931:

"Many complaints of laxness in camps throughout the state and of abuses of prisoners, of improper feeding and of working prisoners in violation of the rules keep coming in; and, as you have seen, the papers are teeming with criticisms made by outsiders touching some of these matters."

And the pathetic letters convicts themselves scrawled laboriously in pencil, pleading letters like Eugene Brown's sent from Gwinnett County on May 2, 1931:

"Mr. E L Reany lissen here Mr Reiny This is Eugne Brown talking Mr Reiney I am begging you with tears in my eyi for a trancefor Becais I cannot make my time here Becais tr. worden and county C B M is beating us over the head wi pick handle and they draw their guns on us and make stand and let these trustes Beat us up and Let the hare gun ti Mr Reiny I dont Belive that you know how they is treatin us prizners you auto cone and see Mr Reiney I want you to do all you can I am willing to go anywhere and make my Time Becais my hand is all messed up and every time I ask the doctor for anything they is ready to punish me my hand is so bad till I cant hardly hold a shurvle and I am asking you now for help I am looking for your awancer wright away Yors

EUGENE BROWN"

I remembered the many, many such letters of abuse and torture from those who "owed Georgia a debt."

I found myself within eight miles of the Seminole County camp and went there again.

A drowsy summer hush was over the stockade. In the glaring light of the day the clapboard shacks baked under the tropic sun. The kitchen with its torn screen, the mess hall with its grease and flies and mosquitoes, the rusty, wire fence and the cross, now bare and bleak, throwing its shadow on the red soil swarming with ants.

A boy lay at the foot of the cross, bound hand and foot, with a pick thrust between the limbs. His eyes were closed and his head lay loose on the soil, as though the neck were broken. He could not move.

He opened his eyes when I walked over to him.

"Does it hurt, boy?" I asked.

"Yes, suh. It sho does," he said weakly and closed his eyes again.

"What did this boy do?" I asked.

"Talked back to a guard," said the warden. "Sometimes they become unconscious and then we untie them," he added.

I examined the neat little booklet of prison rules. Each warden is instructed to "frame in a glass, and hang up in a conspicuous place in the building, a copy of these rules." I did not see them hanging anywhere, nor did the warden have a copy available. But my copy read:

"They [the wardens] shall safely keep all prisoners committed to their custody, rigidly enforce discipline by the of such humane modes of punishment as will best enforce submission to authority. . . ."

"Humane modes of punishment. . . ."

The Commission itself suggests as one humane method of punishing "fastening them in stocks in such a way as will cause them to be restricted in their movements for not longer than one hour at one time, provided the prisoner is found to be physically sound upon examination by the camp physician."

"Stocks," I thought, "this cannot mean the old Puritan stocks for that is gone three hundred years. Even Webster's dictionary says: 'Stocks: a frame of timber, with holes in which formerly the feet and hands of offenders were confined . . . by way of punishment.'"

In the Early County stockade I saw a prisoner in stocks. His hands and feet protruded through the holes made to hold them. I walked closer. I

TORTURE—SOUTHERN STYLE

A prisoner trussed up in a Seminole County (Ga.) chain gang
stockade. He is being punished because he "talked back" to
the guard. He was left under the hot sun until he fainted.

had seen pictures of Puritans in stocks. They sat them on boards in a
public place, but here in Georgia, 300 years later, he did not sit on a board.

He hung, a groaning, helpless, pain-wrenched thing crying weakly:
"O my Lawd, my Lawd, look what they is doin' to Yo' chillun."

He hung, for the board was pulled out from under him, hung three
inches from the ground, with the wood encircling his wrists squeezing
against his arteries and interfering with the circulation while the weight

of the body dragged him down, tearing at his shoulders and threatening to break his back.

The sweat broke out on his face and tears rolled down his cheeks.

"How long do you keep him in stocks?" I asked.

"Not more than an hour at a time," said Warden J. D. Williams. "If they lose consciousness we release them and when they are a little stronger we restrict them again."

"What did he do for this?"

"He's been fussin' about his meals," said the warden.

"Isn't this worse than the lash the legislature abolished?"

"Oh, I don't know. I'd like to see the leather returned. The worst we can give them now is a little stretching."

"Stretching," I thought, "what can this stretching be that is worse than hanging helpless in stocks?"

When you work from sunrise to sunset under a Georgia sun you go mad sometimes and talk back to the guard, and a convict in Early County talked back.

They put handcuffs on him and tied a rope to the cuffs and led him to a little post to which they laced him tightly from ankles to hips. A guard took the rope attached to the handcuffs and swinging it around another post, yanked sharply at the warden's command.

The convict's torso jerked forward, his hands outstretched.

"Pull!" shouted the warden.

The trustee pulled until the rope was taut. He dug his heels into the red clay of the stockade.

The convict screamed in agony.

His head drooped between his outstretched arms.

And as the beads of sweat broke out on his arms and neck and face a cold sweat broke out on me. I doubted my sanity.

They were tearing this convict's arms out!

The guard quickly tied the rope around the post and left him stretched on the Georgia rack while the sun beat upon him and the sweat from his head dripped to the red soil.

Georgia, in this year of our "civilization," 1932, was breaking its convicts on the rack!

I left with the convict's groans ringing in my ears.